ARCANE LEGACY

BOOK 2 OF THE CONDUIT SERIES

FAYE TRASK

OTHER TITLES BY FAYE TRASK

The Conduit Series

Breaking the Bond (Prequel)

Blood Legacy

Keep up-to-date at

www.fayetrask.com

For the silent battles we all fight

CHAPTER
ONE

Kelly dragged her thumb along the aged and battered edge of the envelope for what must have been the thousandth time. Reexamining the words, *Mr. Wainwright* scrawled across the front in ornate black ink. She had memorized every crease, every fiber, every imperfection, looking for some hidden answers. Flipping it over, she slid her fingers across the red wax seal, studying the eight branches with their mismatched prongs and angular symbols that still made no sense to her. She slipped the perfectly fitted card out just enough to reveal the same ornate writing. She didn't need to read it. Just like the envelope, she had memorized every detail.

June 1, 7:00 a.m.
7 Rue de la Chancellerie, Versailles, France
You will find your answers.

Tucking the card back into the envelope, she stuffed it into the pages of a worn leather journal with a frustrated sigh. Her fingers drifted across the smooth cover. The journal had also belonged to Mr. Wainwright. She had discovered it in a box her parents had salvaged from their destroyed retirement home. Her mother didn't know much about him. Only that it was Kelly's ancestor on her father's side. Just like the letter, the journal only left her with more questions.

Slouching back, she could feel the metal ribs of the chair back, pressing hard through the thin cushion. She glared at the journal, irritated by the very sight of it. She forced her attention to the breathtaking skyline.

The bright white lights illuminated the sand-colored limestone of the House of Parliament and Big Ben. She pulled her bathrobe tighter as a gentle breeze passed the Thames. Tugging at the cuff of her sleeve, she paused, then pushed it up. To expose the tattoo-like mark that had become clearer over the past week. She traced its interlocking lines and points with her fingertip. The room of white subway tiles and bloodied weapons returned like a flood in her mind. Jerking her attention away, she pulled the sleeve back down, hugging herself as her heart thumped rapidly with the memory of hopelessness.

Her gaze followed along the historic jagged outline as she forced the memory away. It had been barely a month since she returned home from the military and was struggling to adjust to the quietness of a small town, especially after losing her best friend, Eric. When life was normal.

The rustle of skin on fabric pulled her attention into the hotel room. A man lay sleeping in the bright orange chair at the edge of the bed. His legs stretched out and an original copy of *Frankenstein* open across his bare chest. Drawn in by his nearly perfect pale skin, her eyes lingered on his forearm; a dark red patch in an unclear shape, twisted and pinched at his skin like a burn. Raven-black hair fell like dark curtains, framing his chiseled features, concealing those stunning chocolate eyes had seen straight into her soul —offering the solace and safety to be vulnerable, without fear of rejection. A small smirk tugged at her lips, taking in his physique; even in sleep, he had an aura of power that you didn't see very often anymore. His raw strength radiating from every pore. *The big bad vampire sleeps.*

Turning back to the skyline, she retrieved the pendant from the folds of her bathrobe and let the memory of the night everything changed, the night she met her new friends, replay. The beautiful young redhead she protected at the gas station. She scoffed. *Fiona never needed my help.* The Asylum. The tall, dark, handsome stranger and his friend watching her from across the club. *Now I'm halfway around the world with him.* She took a deep breath, trying to release the knot that had formed in her chest. Vampires. Magic. It's all real. Alexander and his minions interrupted the fond image. The kidnapping; Alexander killing Eric in front of her; Vincent, Dimitri, Maya, and Evalyn each trying to break her will. *For what?*

She twirled the pendant absentmindedly as every moment she was imprisoned replayed in slow motion. Vincent holding the torch to the side of her foot. Maya's face as she jabbed the cattle prod into Kelly's side. She clutched the pendant. Sharp pain shot through her hand. She let the pendant fall back to her chest as she stared at the outline of her hand. Her stomach tightened, remembering the scar on Eric's. The sign of his betrayal but also the faint lines showing his hesitation. For eight months, she had believed that he was dead. Spending countless painful hours arranging his funeral, packing his apartment, trying to figure out what to do next when the biggest part of her life was taken from her. Unaware at the time, she had spiraled into a dark well of depression. Then everything she knew turned on its head when Eric appeared before her, claiming to be a vampire. Kelly sniffed and wiped the forming tear from her eye.

Kelly let out a deep sigh, rubbing her face and the memory of Eric from her mind. As she rested her fingertips on her lips, her gaze landed once again on the journal. A soft thump of a book being closed, followed by bare feet on carpet, sounded behind her.

"There is no more you can learn from it," Theo said, his hand brushing Kelly's hair off to one shoulder.

"There has to be something I missed, something that can tell me what's happening. You can go back to sleep. I will be a bit longer."

"I was not sleeping."

"Oh. You snore like a lumberjack when you're awake then?" Kelly asked.

Theo kissed the curve of her neck, his warm, soft lips a sharp contrast to the coarseness of his newly stubbled cheek.

"I made a promise to watch over you. I keep my promises. Tell me what is wrong."

"Nothing, I'm fine," Kelly said automatically. Theo pulled the remaining chair in front of her and sat looking deep into her eyes, peeling away the lie. She felt that familiar lurch in her chest as her heart skipped a beat.

"I haven't slept well since being held prisoner at Alexander's."

"It is understandable. You need to give yourself time. It was an unimaginable situation."

"It's not that. Sure staring at the corpse of your best friend for days on end doesn't breed mental stability, but it was how easily they entered and manipulated my mind. The one place you feel is yours and yours alone. Why did they even want me? They had a plan but..." Kelly let out a frustrated sigh.

"Unfortunately, manipulating another's mind is not limited to humans. It takes immense skill and years of practice to harness the dark magic required."

"How do we stop it?"

"Training."

"When can we start?"

"After you have rested."

"Resting is a waste of time," she fumed.

"It may feel that way, but you need it, or you will not be capable of the action required." Theo rose, holding out a hand to her. Her eyes fell back to the resplendent skyline.

"I can't."

"There is something else?"

"I can't sleep. Every time I close my eyes, I see her. I see them all. The bloodthirsty snarls, the malevolent scowls, but most of all I see the twisted joy vanishing from Maya's face as I stabbed her."

Theo entered the room, crossing to the duffel bag at the foot of the bed. After rifling through it for a moment, he removed a small stick-like item and returned to his seat, holding it up to her.

"Omari gave this to me before they left. He said it may help."

Kelly took the item from him, rolling it between her fingers for a moment. She smirked.

"He gave this to me before. It was before I could see your true face."

Theo smiled his brilliant white smile, his fangs on full display. Kelly got to her feet and placed it in her mouth like a toothpick. As she chewed, the taste of lavender and honey returned, cradling her in a wave of relaxation. Picking up the journal, they headed inside. She placed it on the nightstand and crawled into the bed. Sitting propped up by pillows, she watched as he returned to his outstretched position and reopened his book.

Her eyes grew heavy, and her mind wandered. *What would life be like with him?* The memory of their first kiss danced into the forefront. The fiery passion, the subtle strength that revealed he would keep her safe at any cost. *But why me?* She lingered on the thought when another wedged its way in. *Love at first sight doesn't exist.* The image of him leaning against his motorcycle now tainted. *It's only infatuation. You are human, there is no future.* A deep sigh escaped her chest. *There is now, that's all that matters.*

"Is that comfortable?" she asked sleepily.

"I have sat in worse places."

"You don't have to sit there. There is plenty of space over here."

"I would not want to intrude on your rest."

"It's a king. It would take not only you but also my bed hog of a dog, Thor, to do that."

Theo smiled, got to his feet, and climbed onto the bed, propping his back against the headboard. Kelly slumped and rested her head on his chest, trying to fight off the effects of the root for just a little longer.

"This is real, right? You and me here?" she asked, uncertainty ebbing in her voice.

"Yes, my darling. This is real." Theo's arm wrapped around her.

"What are we doing tomorrow?" she asked faintly.

"It is 2:18. Do you not mean today?"

"No, tomorrow. Haven't slept yet, so it's still the same day."

Theo chuckled and kissed her head. "On the verge of sleep, you still manage to argue. I must first run an errand, then if you wish, we will see the city. I would like to take you somewhere special tonight."

"Sounds... good," Kelly mumbled as she drifted off to sleep.

THE LATE MORNING sun cascaded in through the balcony curtains. Kelly stirred, burying her face into the darkness her pillow created, not wanting to face the day. The white noise of rushing water splashing against tile that filled the room came to a sudden stop. She brushed the wild strands of chestnut hair from her eyes and spotted Theo pass by the open door, vigorously drying his hair with a towel. Obstructing most of her face with the comforter, she watched as several beads of water trickled the curves of his back.

How can this be real?

She smiled into the blanket. After a few more moments, he emerged from the bathroom, steam still trickling out behind him. She closed her eyes, pretending to still be asleep. Listening to his nearly silent footsteps cross the room, she then felt the pull of the mattress as he sat on the bed. His strong yet gentle hand brushed a few hairs from her face. He stroked his thumb along her cheek. She could feel his weight shift, followed by his hot, minty breath.

"I know you are awake," he whispered.

"Shh no, I'm not," she joked in a whisper.

"You cannot sleep away the day," he chuckled, "I thought you wanted to see the city."

Kelly looked up into his stunning face and felt her heart flutter. Grabbing the edge of the blanket, she tossed it over her head.

"Never!" she giggled.

"The hard way it is," he said, then began grabbing at the lumps of fabric, sending Kelly wriggling and squirming in a fit of laughter.

"Alright, alright, I give, I give!" she said, emerging from her cave.

"Feeling better?" Theo was leaning over her, propped up on one elbow.

"Not really, but I will admit I need a distraction from recent events... and documents." She sighed.

The city didn't matter, and the questions would inevitably work their way back to the forefront of her mind. Staring up at him, the ache of wanting to stay here in this peaceful moment of simple happiness forever formed in her chest. Thrusting her lips to his she kissed him deeply.

"I need a shower," she said, breaking away from him and climbing out of bed. She glanced once more at him before closing the bathroom door.

She pulled her hair into its usual ponytail and gave her outfit a last glance: worn blue jeans and an old loose-fitting Metallica ...*And Justice for All* T-shirt. Four small silver marks just above her elbow poked out from the bottom of her sleeve. The battle between her and Vincent came back in a wave of flashes. He grabbed her so hard, not only digging in his nails, cutting her like razors, but dislocating her shoulder. It was at that moment she knew she was changed as she watched her skin knit itself back together. The questions that she had been obsessing over came creeping back. She placed her hands on the vanity, leaning forward, staring intently into her own stormy blue eyes. "You did what you had to. Bury it. Deal with it some other time. Not today," she whispered through gritted teeth.

As she emerged from the steam-filled bathroom to an empty hotel room, her stomach dropped as the doubt of it being real or a dream pulled at her. The sheer white curtains danced around Theo standing in the doorway to the balcony. A coffee mug in either hand. He smiled, then held one out to her. Taking it from him, Kelly let out a silent sigh of relief as he pressed his lips to her forehead.

"I thought you may be hungry," he said, leading her onto the balcony. On the table was a vibrant array of fresh fruit, pastries and jams, eggs, bacon, juice, and coffee.

"Are we expecting company?" Kelly asked.

"No, why?"

"You ordered enough food for at least four people."

"I may have forgotten how much humans eat. Autumn usually handles that."

"You may not 'eat' but you better help me or I'm not touching a thing."

His lip curled into a smirk. Reaching for the basket of pastries, he retrieved the only cinnamon roll and placed it on the small plate in front of him, then winked at her. She smiled, then served herself a plate. Popping a bite-sized tart into her mouth, she watched him as he read, his stoic expression never wavering. A headline on the front page caught her attention:

TWO MORE MISSING FROM ARCHBISHOP'S PARK, LOCAL AUTHORITIES STRESS VIGILANCE

"Where is Archbishop's Park?" Kelly asked, craning her neck, trying to read more of the article. Theo looked at her, then the article on the front page.

"Not far, just the other side of the hospital," he said, gesturing in its direction.

"Does it seem odd to you?" she asked, her eyebrows drawn together.

"It is hard to say, were they taken against their will, or did they simply wish to leave their current life in search of a new one? Do not dwell on it, darling. I am certain the authorities are doing everything they can," he said, placing a comforting hand on hers.

CHAPTER
TWO

As she stepped onto the sunny street, the modern world fused itself to the historic structures, preserving their proud history. Kelly reached for Theo's hand, interlocking their fingers as she took in the scenery. The focused buzz of the mid-morning commuters encompassed them. A noble stone lion towered above them.

"So, what's the plan?" she asked as they crossed Westminster bridge.

"I need to make one stop then the day is up to you."

"What kind of stop?"

"A quick bite." He smiled.

She glanced up at his eyes hidden behind the dark lenses of his sunglasses. It still felt odd to see him in broad daylight. To her and much of the human population, vampires were creatures of the night who could be fought off with garlic, holy water and killed by sunlight or a stake through the heart. It wasn't until the night she saw Fiona levitating a bottle over Eli's head firsthand that he explained the truth about witches, vampires, and magic.

Vampires weren't killed by sunlight; they were barely harmed by it. It did burn their eyes like a serious sunburn, but as long as they wore sunglasses, they could blend into the daytime masses with little effort. It also made them physically weaker. Still stronger than the average human, but not nearly as strong as they were at night or if they drank human blood.

Theo had pointed out that a stake to the heart could kill anything and he quite enjoyed garlic. On their flight, he told her about the time he spent in Italy and commented on the fact that "if garlic was left out of an Italian dish, it would lose the authenticity."

As for real weaknesses, it was primarily silver, fire and decapitation.

"How far is it?" she asked.

"A couple of streets past the bridge."

Silence fell between them as her mind drifted back to the cabin nestled in a forgotten part of the Maine woods. She was happy to be here with Theo, but part of her missed Autumn, Fiona, and Omari, but mostly Eli. The only human besides her.

"How do you think Eli is doing?" she said, breaking the silence as they crossed the busy street.

"He will be fine. If you would like, you can call him once we return to the hotel."

She worried about Eli. He was such a compassionate person. As an EMT, he was trained to save lives, not take them.

They turned down a narrow one-way street. The brick facades on either side ensnared the essence and timelessness of historic London. As they strolled past a bustling sandwich shop, its doorway overflowing with people, they snaked their way through the throng and ended up standing in front of an abandoned building. The shutters inside the windows were closed and a thin layer of dust could be seen on the inside of the sill. Theo turned the doorknob in the center of the powder blue door and stepped inside. Kelly followed, closing the door behind her. The narrow hall was nothing more than a junction with a door on each side and a set of stairs at the end. Theo had reached the stairs and disappeared down them. When she caught up to him, he was in front of a large metal door at the bottom of the stairs. Theo knocked once, paused, then knocked again. A hidden panel slid to one side, revealing a pair of hazel eyes. They locked onto Theo's, then flicked to Kelly.

"Brought a snack?" a deep gravelly voice groaned from behind the door.

"She is with me and none of your concern," Theo warned.

The man's eyes darted to Kelly again, and his thick eyebrows wrinkling in disgust. *Can he tell I am human?* The small panel snapped shut, followed by a loud clunk, then the door opened. Through the doorway, she glanced at the guard. He was large, around the same height as Theo, and nearly double in girth. His long, curly black hair was collected in a disheveled ponytail at the base of his neck. The wild strands intertwined with his long crumb-speckled beard. As Kelly passed, the guard's disgust shifted to an animal-like vigilance, flashing a yellow-tinged fang. Kelly gripped Theo's hand. *What was that all about?* They continued to the end of a narrow hall where it opened to a small waiting room.

The outdated pastel green wallpaper clashed with the worn red fabric and wooden frame of the chairs that surrounded the room. Several occupants were scattered throughout, flipping through old magazines and browsing the sunglass tower in the corner. On the opposite side of the room, there was a large reception window. A woman a little shorter than Kelly stood talking to the comely receptionist. As they made their way to the reception desk, the air shifted. The hair on Kelly's neck stood on end. She glanced around. Everyone was staring at them. The couple closest to her moved from their seats to a pair of open ones on the other side of the room, each with the same look the guard had given her. The woman talking with the receptionist turned and let out a small gasp, averting her gaze as she darted past them and hurried out of the waiting room.

The same vigilance flicked across the receptionist's face before being replaced with a smile as they approached the window, her fangs a startling pearl white. Her platinum blonde hair curled in loose rings that flowed down the center of her back, vibrant blue eyes were accentuated even more by the matching baby blue dress that clung tight around her chest displaying a modest amount of cleavage then flowed out gracefully. A delicate jingle sounded through the air as she tucked one of her golden locks behind her ear.

"Well, hey there, darlin', it's been a while. How ya doin'?" Her American southern drawl caught Kelly off guard more than anything else.

"Good afternoon, Angel, I need a delivery to the hotel." Theo smiled.

"How much you looking to git?"

"A week's worth and one for the road," he said, placing a flask on the counter.

"Sure thing." She winked flirtatiously at him, then tapped away at the old keyboard. Kelly clenched her jaw, jealousy surging in her chest. *She's just being nice. Calm down. What is wrong with me?* She scanned the room to ignore it. Heat rose in her throat. *Why was everyone on edge? Is Theo more dangerous than I realize?*

A man entered the waiting room, his shoulder-length dirty blond hair held back by thick Oakley sunglasses on top of his head. His rugged features scratched at her mind. There was something familiar about his broad square jaw, which was covered in a short, darker beard flecked with gray. His dark red leather jacket complemented the plain black T-shirt underneath.

"Tank?" The man's deep dulcet voice added to the gnawing feeling in her mind.

"How are you, my friend?" Theo responded in delight; they shook hands, pulling each other into a one-armed hug. The man's attention transferred to Kelly, his forehead crinkling for a moment, then returned to its excited state.

"Oh man, last time I saw this guy was '84 in Las Cruces just after Jimmy and the guys got called back for their encore," he said to Kelly.

"He always hated you calling him Jimmy," Theo laughed.

"Where the hell did you go man? You missed one killer after party."

Their conversation became a muddle of noise as Kelly's mind searched for why he seemed so familiar. *There is something about him. How I have never met him before, yet...*

"I would like to introduce you to—"

"Kelly," she said, extending her hand.

"A pleasure to meet you, Wyatt—"

"Sim!" she finished, finally placing his face. "The lead guitarist and vocalist of Anarch."

"You're a fan?" he asked.

"Little bit," she said. *I guess the vampire rumor wasn't just a publicity thing.*

"You're all set, darlin'," Angel, the receptionist, said. Theo thanked her, then stepped away from the counter.

"It was great to see you, old friend."

"Don't tell me you gotta go, it's been too long, we need to catch up," Wyatt groaned.

"Maybe some other time. I promised Kelly some sightseeing," Theo said.

"First time in London?"

"Yes," Kelly smirked, trying to contain her elation.

"If you are interested, we are playing at Delirium tonight. Why don't you come?"

Theo turned to Kelly. "It is up to you."

"It sounds great."

"Excellent," Wyatt exclaimed, his smile stretching to his cool gray eyes. They shook hands again, then Theo and Kelly made their way out of the room, back down the narrow hall and onto the street.

"If you truly wish to go, then we need to make another stop."

"What for?"

"Clothes," Theo said.

"What's wrong with what I brought?" Kelly asked.

"Delirium is a club with a very specific clientele, and you dress a little too..." He paused, searching for the word.

"Manly? American?" she offered.

"Human," he said with a smirk. "I believe there is a store a few streets over that will suit your needs."

They walked in silence as Theo weaved them down this street and that. Kelly noticed the trendy window displays or change in brick facades as they passed, her gaze fixated on the pavement. Her chest tightened again as she pictured the receptionist with her polished appearance and Southern belle demeanor. Her stomach squirmed like a pit of angry snakes, their venom creeping its way to her brain. *Who am I kidding? I'm human, he's an immortal vampire, there isn't a future for us. Why did I think this was a good idea?* Theo turned down a dark alleyway between two busy streets, stopping in the middle. Lost in thought, she bumped into him.

"Shit, sorry," she apologized, glancing up. Her eyes darted from his dark sunglasses to the base of his neck. She didn't want that penetrating gaze to dig its way into her mind, peeling back her defenses and examining the insecurities she had buried. He removed his sunglasses and slid a finger under her chin, turning her face to his.

"You mean more to me than words can express, and no one can take that away. Do you understand?" he said, flashing her a reassuring smile. *How did he know? Is my insecurity that obvious?* She couldn't help but mirror it. Her cheeks flushed, he brought his lips to hers and kissed her deeply. The angry squirming in her stomach released instantly, replaced with every intangible thought.

A few feet ahead stood an arched opening, its two large black doors were propped open more for aesthetic than use. A smaller set of doors embedded with panes of wrinkled glass on its top half complemented the remaining solid black wood.

Theo pushed on the door; an electronic tone sounded as they crossed the threshold. Kelly gawked at the exposed brick walls covered from floor to ceiling in various articles of gothic clothing. Everything from crimson red corsets and black vinyl pants to heavy metal band t-shirts and lace underwear. The music tied the mood of the store together with its screaming vocals being drowned out by the blaring guitar and thundering double bass. A gangly woman in red plaid pants and a black corseted halter top with dyed black and red hair stood at the top of a ladder in the back of the store hanging some new men's tops.

"How's it goin'?" the woman said, smiling brightly climbing off the ladder. Kelly's eyes were drawn to the woman's bold makeup, her white skin a shocking contrast against her dramatic eyeliner and bright red lipstick. She noticed a small red puncture wound poking out from a tight-fitting black collar around the woman's neck. There was a golden name tag pinned to the collar that said "Rachel" in black letters. "Need some 'elp with anyfin'?"

"I need a new outfit, I guess," Kelly said, still not convinced she did.

"Club Delirium," Theo added, handing her a gold credit card. Rachel's gaze landed on Theo's mouth; her expression changed from the fake helpful grin all customer service had to one of true excitement. She scurried to the front of the store, locked it.

"Right," she said, spinning around. "So, what we thinking?" She looked at each of them. Kelly shrugged. Rachel paused for a moment, then scanned Kelly from head to toe, circling her several times before stopping. Theo smirked, slinking off to the front of the store.

"I bet you would look well fit in this mini and a black and red corset," she squealed, her eyes wide as she grabbed items off the nearest rack. "Y'know, show the world what God gave yer," she winked at Kelly.

"No," Kelly said more abruptly than she had meant. The memory of Alexander dressing her like some doll came flooding back. Rachel stood silent, part offended and part in shock that a woman didn't want a short, flirtatious skirt.

"I don't like wearing skirts and I'm not a fan of the restricted movement corsets have," Kelly clarified.

"He'll do all the moving if you wear that," she said, hushed, jerking her head toward Theo, who found a chair at the front of the store. Kelly's face went flush. Her eyes darted to him just in time to see him lift the magazine to cover his large grin.

"Do you have any jeans?" Kelly asked. Looking crestfallen for a moment, the woman then perked up and dragged Kelly across the store. They crisscrossed through the store, and after what felt like an eternity, Kelly and Rachel brought all her items to the register and boxed them.

"Please have them sent to the hotel," Theo said, joining them at the register.

"Absolutely, sir. Is there anything else today? We do have additional services for our select clientele," she said in a breathy tone, sliding a slim black menu across the counter to him. He at it, then slid the menu to Kelly.

She glanced at the menu. At the top, large gold letters read "PACKAGES"; then beneath were four options written in their corresponding colors: Opal, Carnelian, Aventurine, and Citrine. She flipped the menu over, looking for a description of each, but there was none. Returning to the options, she looked at the color each was written in: Opal in a pearlescent white, Carnelian in fiery orange with traces of red, Aventurine in luminescent jade green, and Citrine in yellowish gold. She raked over it several times before choosing.

"Carnelia, looks nice, I guess."

THREE

"Come in," Theo said, opening the hotel room door.

Rachel stepped into the room with a large, rolling black case. She spotted Kelly standing near the bathroom. Rachel pushed her inside and closed the door behind them.

"Right, let's put your face on," Rachel said, flicking open the locks of her case.

"I'm sorry? What are you doing here?"

"The Carnelia package," she answered, as if it explained everything. The blank stare on Kelly's face told the woman otherwise. "First time at Delirium, I am assuming?"

"Yes."

"Well, the customers of Delirium are a little... different," Rachel said, wrinkling her nose.

"Vampires, you mean."

"And you're human?"

"I'm not seeing your point."

"The more yer look like one of them, the less they'll notice ya. If you go in like this," she waved her hand, gesturing at Kelly's normal look, "they will peg you for human straight away. Even try to lure you into some dark corner. If you look like one of them, they take that as a sign that you are claimed."

"Claimed?" Kelly echoed.

"Uh huh, by one of them. Like that dish out there," she said in a suggestive tone.

"I'm not claimed. I am not a piece of luggage. The fact that I am actually going with him doesn't show that?"

"Afraid not. I'm not fond of the possessive standing vampires adhere by but in this case, it could mean the difference of life and death."

Kelly clenched her teeth. She spent years proving that women were just as capable as men, they could hold their own, and now it felt like it was being ripped away. Even if it was only for one night.

Rachel flipped open the top of her case; the inside was filled with makeup, hair spray, and a million different styling products Kelly hadn't seen before. Rachel began working away at Kelly's hair, blabbing on about this and that. What tourist sites were a scam, and which were worth it? Kelly's mind kept returning to Alexander's mansion and Evalyn pulling and teasing her hair in a similar manner. Her heart climbed to her throat. *It's not the same, you are safe. It's not the same, Theo is in the next room. You are safe.*

"Alright, love?" Rachel asked.

"Yeah, I'm... fine."

"You can tell me, it's just us girls," she said, trying to sound comforting.

"Are you..."

"Human? Aye," Rachel finished.

"Do you have to..."

"Blend in? Kind of, this is my regular look but mostly

it's because I work at the store, so I get to go to Delirium whenever and no one bothers me."

"Oh," Kelly said, falling silent as Rachel finished styling her hair, then moved on to Kelly's makeup. When she was finished, she packed up her things and reached for the door.

"Have fun tonight. Maybe I'll see you there. Cheers," she said, closing the door behind her.

Kelly changed into a pair of black jeans that had been ripped up and frayed around the edges that she could fight in. She wasn't too sure about the top Rachel had picked out—it exposed lots of skin with its large neckline and thick lace detailing, but Rachel also provided her with an accompanying black bandeau. Rachel styled Kelly's hair in a half-up style and did her makeup to create smoky eyes. To complete the gothic look.

Kelly stared at her reflection in amazement; before meeting Theo, she would never have worn anything so exposing, but now she felt just as strong and sure of herself as she would in her favorite sweatshirt. There was another knock at the hotel room door.

"This arrived while you were out," the hotel employee said.

"Thank you," Theo replied, then closed the door. Kelly opened the bathroom door to Theo holding an envelope nearly identical to the one from Jonas's journal. He slid his thumb under the flap, lifting the wax seal and retrieving the letter inside.

"What is that?"

"Nothing that cannot be dealt with later," he said, stuffing the letter back in the envelope. He turned to her and froze. "You are—" he stared, at a loss for words.

"Is it too much? I'll pay you back. Rachel said this is how everyone looks."

"Absolutely breathtaking," Theo finished. Kelly fought back a smile, then crossed to him and pecked him on the cheek. "I would not dream of taking a dime. It is a gift."

"You like it then?"

"Very much. It is almost a shame we have plans," he joked. Her heart hammered in her chest, wanting to break free from its cage. He snaked his arm around her waist, pulling their bodies together. "Of course, we could always cancel."

"I think your friend would be mad."

"He is a vampire. He can wait."

"You're a vampire, you can wait," she mocked him. "Who was the letter from?"

"Autumn. The council has returned with a date for Fiona's case. It is in two days."

"That's good, isn't it?"

"Not always, unless she has a good defense; she could get into serious trouble."

"But she did it to save my life."

Theo dropped onto the end of the bed, leaning on his knees. His eyes were on the floor, but his focus was on Paris with Fiona and his family. Her insides gnawed at her, seeing him this way.

"How do we help her?"

"You would have to be there. Give a statement to the council and even then, they still may not be lenient." He ran his fingers through his hair as if wiping away the concern buried inside, then stood. "Do not worry about it now. Let us go and enjoy the evening. As I said before, we can deal with this later."

She wrapped her arms around his neck. Fiona was like a sister to him; Kelly could only imagine what was going through his mind. She pecked him on the cheek, then smiled.

"What is it?"

"You don't use contractions."

He looked at her, puzzled.

"You say do not instead of don't. It's cute."

"I never noticed. Don't worry," he said, as if feeling out the words, then shaking his head as if doing so had left a bad taste in his mouth. Kelly, pleased she had distracted him, smiled. Theo's expression softened, mirroring her smile in thanks.

THE NIGHTTIME STREETS of London had a different energy to them than before. The air was wilder and heavier, with a lawless desire. Theo led her once again, weaving down the honeycomb of busy streets and empty alleyways. They turned a corner. Not far ahead was a tunnel lit with color-changing lights that pulsed along with the loud dance music echoing out into the night. Kelly reached for Theo's hand as they neared its entrance.

The walls and ceiling were covered in graffiti on top of graffiti, every artist adding their own touch to one miraculous piece of art. A large crowd was reeling and writhing as one to the music. The DJ mixing seamlessly into the next track. At the middle of the tunnel, Theo steered Kelly to a metal door hidden among the art and pounded on it. The door was opened by a stocky, well-built man dressed in all black. As it closed with a metal *thunk*, the dance music from the tunnel was replaced with muffled melodic heavy metal. They continued down a narrow set of stairs, then stopped in front of a pair of black graffiti-covered doors. Theo turned to Kelly, tucking a small strand of hair behind her ear, his fingers caressing her jawline.

"I am sorry we did not get to see the city today."

"It's okay, we still have tomorrow, right?"

"Right. Once we enter, do not leave my side."

"Am I not safe?"

"Yes, as long as you stay with me, some vampires do not care about ownership. If we get separated for any reason, find Wyatt. He will keep you safe until I find you."

"But that won't happen, right?" she said, as a small tremble slipped out.

"Right," he agreed.

She paused, thinking about the last time she was in a room filled with vampires and the letter about Fiona's trial. She glanced at her hands, then fidgeted, picking at the sides of her nails.

"Darling, look at me," he cooed. Reluctantly, she looked up, connecting with his large brown eyes that could penetrate any wall or mask she could create. "For tonight, our world only exists here and now. You are safe with me. Everything else can wait."

"I think I can handle that," Kelly said wryly.

He grabbed the door handle and pulled it open for her. She smiled up at him and stepped through.

The room was larger than it appeared. A large group was forming in the center of the dance floor, waiting for the show to start. The booths along the walls were shrouded in darkness only lit by the single candle placed in the center of the small table, its wrapped bench the same color as the pomegranate curtains that were pulled to either side. A curvaceous woman in a short and tight leopard print dress was leading an exceedingly pale, lanky man in black leather pants and fishnet shirt into one of the booths. The man glanced at the woman's ass and bit his lip, then glanced over at Theo and Kelly. His expression changed to a grimace as he scanned Kelly. She swallowed hard, averting her eyes only to notice several more people stopping and staring at her the same way. The memory of the vampires at Alexander's mansion took hold. A knot formed in her throat; she became rooted to the spot yet ready to act at a moment's notice as her heart rammed against her ribs.

As she glanced around the room, Kelly saw Rachel gesturing excitedly, guiding her date toward them. He was only a little taller than her and his long, light brown hair had slipped out of its ponytail, making his disgruntled look even more menacing. His arm slid around her neck as they approached.

"So what ya think?" Rachel shouted over the music. Kelly put on an enthusiastic face and gave Rachel an approving thumbs-up. Rachel looked elated to be speaking, when the man cut her off by whispering something in her ear. Kelly noticed a shadow cross Rachel's features, only to be replaced with that practiced customer service smile she had perfected. With a wave, the man took her away toward the bar where another man was waiting. Kelly watched as Rachel's date held out his hand to greet him. He seemed just as intimidating as Rachel's companion, and part of the tattoo on his arm caught Kelly's eye. *Exsurgat diabolus.* The two men glanced over at Kelly.

Should I be ready for a fight? Theo's arm snaked around her waist.

"You are safe. I have you. They are about to start," he whispered, weaving them closer to the stage.

Even over the wailing guitar, it was as if they were back in the quiet of their hotel room. She took a deep, steadying breath and followed as he led them through the crowd. The band played the final chords of their song and left the stage. Theo found a spot near the stage and pulled Kelly in front of him. The excitement she had felt earlier when they met Wyatt crept its way back. Theo slid his arms around her waist. She leaned her head back, resting it on his chest. Closing her eyes, she pictured the room exactly as it was, then began erasing the people around them, dimming the lights until there was only one light that silhouetted them, and soon everyone was gone, and it was only the two of them as they were.

A tumultuous roar shattered her calm state, her eyes shooting open in time to see Anarch take the stage. First out was Zeke, the rhythm guitarist, his dark hair gelled back neatly. The black tank top he wore clung to his built physique, much like the tight red leather pants and black studded belt. Kelly couldn't help but squirm, something settling in her stomach. In the photos of the band, he always gave off the genuine nice guy, look but here in person, it was arrogant and malicious. Directly behind him was Kyle, the drummer, a slender, bare-chested man with a bright blue mohawk and red plaid pants, the male equivalent to Rachel's outfit from earlier. Followed by Wyatt, still in the same pants as before, his sleeveless fishnet shirt was covered by a holey black and white Motörhead shirt that had its sleeves and most of the sides cut off. Last on was Hunter, the bassist, the sides of her head were shaved creating a crown of hair that she had formed into long black dreadlocks stopped at the shoulder of her white fishnet shirt, her matching white pants covered in chains and deliberate tears showing her darker complexion.

An ear-splitting wail came from Wyatt's guitar; his hands moved with a speed only few humans could come close to. Zeke, Hunter, and Kyle all joined in creating the familiar music Kelly would blast at home in her garage or navigating the winding back roads.

"How you doing tonight, Delirium!" Wyatt called into the microphone. The crowd roared in response. "We got something special for you tonight off our new album 'Down in Flames' out this Friday. Here is 'She Said He's the Devil'." The band played the melodic intro, then Wyatt sang into the mic, the lyrics entrancing the crowd as they ebbed and flowed along with the music.

She said he's the devil in disguise
Pulling her into the dark of the night
With the touch of his lips
He consumes her

By the end of their set the energy in the room became palpable, setting Kelly on edge. In a human crowd, it would be a sense of euphoria, but here, one wrong move, and it would be a bloodbath.

"You guys have been an amazing audience. Let's hear it for who you actually came to see. The 69 Eyes!" The crowd's roar surged again; this time, a few shrill voices could be heard above the others. As the band left the stage, Wyatt's gaze connected with Theo's. Wyatt jerked his head in the direction they were heading, and Theo responded with a nod.

"What was that about?" Kelly shouted, barely able to be heard over the crowd.

"He has invited us backstage."

"Are we going?"

"Only if you wish it."

"Do we have to go right now, or can we wait?" she asked. He smiled in response.

The 69 Eyes had taken the stage, playing one of Kelly's favorite songs. As they swayed to the music, Theo bent his head and sang into her ear; his voice was just as velvety as when he spoke. She faced him, pressing their foreheads together. The lyrics wrapped in his dulcet tones flowed directly into her, giving the words more meaning than they ever could from someone else.

The calm image returned, washing over her, lost in their own world. The roar of the crowd once again pulled them out of the peace. Kelly looked into Theo's eyes; they had turned from their beautiful light brown to a deeper shade—next would be black. He needed to feed soon. She smiled, giving him a quick nod. He pressed his lips to her forehead. Theo's fingers interlocked with hers. He weaved them through the crowd to a door that read "musicians only."

Slipping through the door, they entered a hall lined with doors on either side. They followed the explosion of laughter to an open door. Wyatt was leaning against the large vanity engrossed in his conversation with Hunter, who straddled the armrest of the couch, describing what appeared to be a fight with a drunk that tried to get handsy with her. Kyle was sitting in an old metal chair balancing on its back two legs with a towel draped over his head.

"Hey, you made it! Awesome!" Wyatt exclaimed. Hunter lifted her drink in greeting. "How did you like the set?"

"You guys were amazing," Kelly gushed. Wyatt grabbed a CD and a silver Sharpie from the vanity top. He scribbled his signature, then passed it to Hunter. Opening the small refrigerator tucked under the vanity, he handed a dark bottle to Theo and a water to Kelly.

"We heard about what happened with Alexander. Fabian is pissed. He wants answers."

"Who's Fabian?" Kelly asked.

"Fabian is the vampires' consul to the Council," Theo answered. Hunter tossed the CD, hitting Kyle in the chest, then the pen, catching him off guard. Losing his balance, his chair tumbled back, launching his cup into the air, spilling the contents down Kelly's front. The warm blood hit her skin. Kelly's body went rigid as she glanced around the room; the air became thick with an animalistic tension. Theo positioned himself between the band and Kelly.

"We're cool, right guys?" Wyatt boomed. It was more of a statement than a question. Hunter and Kyle both nodded, wrestling back their desire to feed.

"I'm sorry," Kyle apologized, getting to his feet.

"It's okay, I'm fine, just a little... blood. Er, where is the bathroom?" she grabbed the towel from the floor and began wiping her front.

"Third door on the right," Wyatt said, grabbing another dark bottle from the fridge and tossing it to Kyle.

"That's why we use bottles."

"Yeah, yeah," Kyle replied, as if this were the thousandth time he had been told.

Kelly left the room, continuing to clean the blood. *I feel like Carrie on prom night.* She turned the handle and pushed the door open. Loud moans pulled Kelly's attention away from the cold patches of smeared blood.

A mountain of flesh and fabric was writhing before her. The curvaceous woman was propped on the vanity table, her dress bunched around her waist, the thin shoulder strap by her elbow exposing her large perky breasts partially blocked by a head of black hair. Her manicured nails drawing blood from the man's muscular pale back. Her legs wrapped around his waist; his red leather pants only pulled to his knees.

"Shit, er, sorry," Kelly stuttered, closing the door. The

heavy panting, punctuated with moans and grunts of pleasure, continued behind the door. She looked down the hall. *Shit, that was left, not right.* Crossing the hall, she opened the door cautiously.

The bathroom was a glorified closet with only the basics: a toilet, sink, mirror, a stack of paper towels, and an overflowing trash bin. The walls mimicked the tunnel above, covered in layers of graffiti, old show posters, and some black Sharpie that read "for a good time call" or "blood donations accepted" and phone numbers beneath.

Kelly locked the door behind her. The knobs squeaked as water poured from the tap. Peeling off the lace top, she dampened a wad of paper towels and began cleaning the blood from her front. *I guess this was a good outfit, after all.* Once her skin was clean, she tossed the bloodstained wad into the trash and ran her top under the water, guiding it back and forth, watching the water go from diluted red to clear. Her shirt and the basin became a blur as her face suddenly burned and a wave of dizziness washed over her. She clutched the sink to steady herself. Blindly, she grabbed a paper towel, wetted it and pressed it against one cheek, then the other. *What the fuck?* She took several deep breaths as the room came back into focus. Turning off the tap, she wrung the last bit of water from her top.

Goose bumps ran across her skin as she slid the damp lace top back on. Checking her reflection once more for any missed blood before heading back to Theo, a bright white piece of paper pasted on the back of the door caught her eye. Large, bold red letters read "MISSING." Below it was a black-and-white photo she assumed was a few years old, judging by the person's long emo-styled bangs sweeping over one eye, lip piercing, and the strange glasses that reminded her of house shutters. Below the photo had the words "HAVE YOU SEEN THIS MAN?" followed by their name, age, some identifying marks, and the date and location they were last seen. She scanned over the poster several times, trying to commit the name and face to memory just in case. *Chris Bradtree, 20. Poor kid, I hope he made it home.* Her eyes fell to the date last seen *six months ago.* Her heart ached for his loved ones. She pulled open the bathroom door and headed back to the band's green room.

Theo stepped into the hall as a woman's giggle filled the air behind her. Kelly turned back to see the woman from before—a tall, jaw-droppingly gorgeous woman in a tight, dusty pink sequin and lace cocktail dress. She turned down the hall, heading for the exit on the other side of Theo. Zeke followed, crossing into the bathroom. The woman's plunging neckline and high hemline oozed temptation and desire. She ran her matching pink nails through her long platinum blond hair and stopped next to Theo and Kelly.

"My, my, Theodore, you look better every time I see you," she said, touching his bicep.

"Gabriella," Theo responded curtly, jerking away from her.

"Still as hard as I remember. We used to have a lot of fun. You and me. Do you remember?" She leaned close to his ear. "When you're ready for a real woman, you know where I am," she said in a whisper loud enough for Kelly to hear.

Gabriella's gaze flitted to Kelly, her cold steel eyes digging into her confidence. "Like what you see?" She flashed Kelly a seductive wink, then sashayed down the hall as if gliding. The electric tension between Theo and Gabriella set Kelly on edge. She fought back a snarl. *Who is she? Why am I ready to fight her? I'm not the jealous type... or am I?*

"I was coming to see if everything was alright," Theo said to Kelly.

"Who was that?"

"No one." His harsh tone eased once Gabriella had gone.

"Besides being covered in blood like some horror movie, then walking in on people having sex, yeah, I'm fine," Kelly smirked.

"You do not need to lie to me," he said.

"Getting covered in blood tends to dampen the mood."

"Does it?" he asked.

"For humans it does."

"You were in the mood before?"

"I was having a good night. Why do men assume that expression means sex?"

"I was only joking."

"Actually, I'm kind of worn out. If you want to stay, you can. I think I can make it back to the hotel on my own." Kelly let out a deep sigh.

"Then we will leave. I would rather my time be spent with you."

"But what about your friends?"

"We are vampires. It is only a matter of time before we see each other again." He shrugged off his leather jacket and draped it over her shoulders. She pulled it closed, wrapping herself in his lingering essence. She inhaled deeply, amber and citrus, her favorite.

CHAPTER
FOUR

As the hotel room door closed behind them, Kelly hung Theo's jacket on the chair by the door and sat to remove her shoes. Her feet sighed in relief as she arranged them neatly next to the chair. Theo had kicked off his shoes, placing them next to hers, then pulled off his shirt when there was a knock on the door. He opened then promptly closed the door, holding another envelope. He thumbed it open, removed the letter, then crossed to the hotel phone and dialed.

"British Airways ticket counter, please."

"What's going on? Where are you going?" Kelly crossed to him.

"I need two tickets on the next flight to Paris, France."

"Theo, what is going on?"

"When does it depart?"

"Theo, answer me!" she shouted. He continued to ignore her while trying to book the tickets. Kelly pressed the hook switch on the phone base, cutting the call. Theo lifted his gaze from the floor to Kelly's. She gnawed on the inside of her cheek, immediate regret swelling in her chest. She refused to be ignored, and she wouldn't go somewhere without knowing what the hell had him acting this way.

"Fabian," he answered.

"The head vampire? What about him?"

"He has requested to speak with me. I can only assume it is regarding Alexander."

"Why can't you call him or just talk to him when we go for Fiona's trial?"

"He is the consul; he does not wait. If he calls on you, you are to report immediately and without hesitation, no matter the situation."

"We are supposed to be on vacation. You know, decompressing."

Theo sighed and pinched at the bridge of his nose. "Did you not want to go to Versailles?"

Kelly's stomach dropped. *7 Rue de la Chancellerie, Versailles, France.* The elegant scrawled address burned in her mind. She sat next to him on the bed. He handed her the envelope with the letter. She scanned the short message, then turned her attention to the envelope. The wax seal was the same fork-pronged wheel as the letter from Jonas's journal.

"This symbol."

"It is the Council's seal."

"Why didn't you tell me this when I showed you the letter in the journal?" she asked. Theo didn't answer. A tense silence filled the air between them. Kelly clenched her teeth so hard pain shot through her jaw, her skin turning hot as her blood raced to her cheeks. She got up from the bed and stepped out onto the balcony, letting the gentle breeze cool her. *Was it a mistake? Traveling with someone I just met halfway across the world, hoping I would find answers to questions I can't even put into words.* She gripped the railing, the cold steel sending a cascade of goose bumps up her arms. There was a soft click. She could feel his warm energy as he stood behind her.

"I must go and speak with Fabian. We can still have our vacation in Versailles."

Kelly turned, glaring up at him. The minute her eyes connected with his, her anger faltered and the thought of going became more bearable. He leaned against the railing and pulled her in front of him. He brushed her cheek with his thumb, then rested his hands on her hips.

"I am sorry. I cannot explain it for you to understand."

"No, I understand. I just..." she broke off. "Why didn't you tell me you recognized the seal?"

"I did not think it relevant."

"Not relevant! They probably know what happened to me. They could have the answers I'm looking for," she snapped.

"How about I make it up to you? What do you say to dinner? I know this charming little restaurant in Versailles."

"Like a date?" she blurted.

"Yes, a date, our first date, if you will."

"Then what would flying here, going shopping and Delirium fall under?"

"Errands," he responded nonchalantly, flashing his knee-weakening smile.

"Okay, it's a date."

Theo pulled her hips toward him, causing her to stumble into his chest. She placed her arm around his neck, running her fingers through his hair. He kissed her deeply, wrapping his arms around her waist, pulling her closer. Her anger continued to melt as she mirrored the desire his body radiated. His lips traveled to the curve of her neck, then broke away.

"We must get going. The next flight leaves soon."

CHAPTER
FIVE

They weaved their way through the empty airport, heading toward the exit. Rounding a corner, the line of rental counters sat unattended. A largely built man in a black suit stood by the exit. Theo approached and without a word, the man jerked his head in a nod, then took both their bags and led them to a black Bentley waiting for them. The man placed their bags in the trunk while another opened the door. Theo rounded the other side of the car. The crimson interior caught her off guard as she slipped into the seat. Between the unbelievably supple leather and the shape of the seat cradling her, Kelly shifted uncomfortably, heat rising in her throat as the memories of Alexander's wealth came surging back. Theo slinked his hand across the black wooden veneer of the center console over to hers and interlocked their fingers. She glanced down at their hands and began to relax.

"Drink?" Theo asked, gesturing to the crystal decanter and matching glasses displayed in its own custom holder. Kelly gently shook her head. Turning to face the window, her eyes landed on the headrest and the council's symbol embroidered into it.

The car left the parking lot and barreled down the highway. The darkened landscape flew past in a blur of flickering orange and black.

"Sleep. I will wake you when we arrive."

She smiled weakly at him, then slumped in her seat and rested her head back, staring blankly out the window, hoping it would lull her into a hypnotic sleep. Absentmindedly gliding her thumb along the edge of the journal hidden in her jacket.

Half an hour later, the car came to a stop at a set of faded sky-blue doors. Kelly straightened up and followed Theo's lead as he climbed out.

"Are we here? Is this the Council?"

"Not quite. The door is up ahead," Theo said, then headed down the joining street.

"If this isn't the door, why did they leave us here? Why not take us straight to it?" Kelly asked, catching up to him. Theo pointed at a street sign marked "one way."

"Though the Council has been here for centuries, we had to disguise the entrance to keep the location secret."

"Okay, but where are they going? They have our stuff?"

"Do not worry, there is an underground garage they use; our bags are fine."

In the dim orange glow of the streetlight, she could make out a set of red doors large enough for a truck to drive through. Next to it was a set of three small steps with a smaller matching door tucked into an alcove at the top. Theo led the way up the steps and through the door. As she crossed the threshold, she noticed the council seal carved into the door's stone frame.

They followed along a short hallway before entering a

large lobby with a desk placed in between two old-fashioned elevator doors. The small woman at the desk had a dark brown pixie cut that framed her round face. She glanced up, flashed a brilliant white smile, then returned to what she was doing. They approached the elevator to the right. Once they were both inside, Theo slid the metal cage closed and pulled the lever. Kelly caught what the woman had been looking at so intently, Casablanca was playing on her computer.

The elevator creaked and groaned as it continued downward. A light ding sounded as they came to a stop. They stepped out into a large atrium with white marble pillars and matching floors that partially climbed the eggnog-painted walls. The small golden accents were tasteful and less self-serving than Alexander's decor had been. The farther they got from the elevator, the more the room opened to a domed ceiling made of glass, artificial light pouring in. At the base of the dome, large golden letters read:

Astra inclinant; sed non obligant

"The stars incline us; they do not bind us," a familiar voice came from behind them. Kelly whirled around. A tall, sensual woman in a lavender sundress approached. Her long raven hair accentuated her glowing golden skin as it flowed in gentle waves to her waist.

"Autumn!"

"Hello, dear. How have you been? Are you enjoying your vacation?" She beamed.

"I was, up until a couple hours ago." She shot a sideways glance at Theo.

"Have you seen Fabian?" Theo asked Autumn.

"Yes, he just left the high council chamber. He should be heading to his office."

"I will find you when I am finished." Theo gave Kelly a quick peck on the cheek, then darted off down one of the connecting hallways. Autumn slinked her arm around Kelly's, leading her in the opposite direction.

"How was London? Did you get to do much sightseeing?"

"No, actually, we didn't get to see anything outside of Club Delirium," she said, stifling a yawn.

"Tired?"

"Yeah, haven't really slept much," Kelly said, trying to rub the tiredness from her eyes.

"I'm sure. It has been some time. So, I'm told." A pleasant smile crept across Autumn's face.

"What? No, not... You said we would talk about what happened to me at Alexander's. How my cell door blew the door off its hinges as if it was nothing. How and why I healed so fast. What this mark is on my arm?" Peppered with frustration, the words poured from her like a dam breaking from the weight of water behind it.

"Shh, we will talk later. I'm sure you would like to change and relax." She stopped in front of a wooden door with a large pane of frosted glass set in.

"You aren't just saying that, right? We are going to figure out what happened. What's going on?" she asked, annoyance bubbling in her gut.

"Yes, but not until you are well rested."

"A shower would be nice," Kelly sighed as a wave of exhaustion took hold. She rolled the edge of her shirt between her fingers and a stiff patch of dried blood.

"I made sure your bag was immediately brought here once you arrived. There is a bathroom and a bed for you.

You are safe here. I will come back for you in a couple hours."

Closing the door, she lightly tapped the window, praying its fragile appearance was only a deception. Then made sure the door was locked before turning her attention to the rest of the room. It was small and sparsely furnished. She slipped off her leather jacket and tossed it on the twin bed that was pushed to one side with clean sheets taunting her to climb in, at its foot was her duffle bag and a stack of towels with hotel-sized shampoo, conditioner, and lotion. *Hotel de Council*. She scoffed, then drifted over to the bathroom. It wasn't much bigger than two phone booths pushed together, its small white tiles stretched from ceiling to floor. Inside the door was a mirror hanging over a porcelain pedestal sink, directly next to that a matching porcelain toilet. She stared at the shower curtain bunched up against the wall. Her gaze followed along its track to the showerhead attached to the wall, then to the floor. A single drain set in the center. This was far from a modern hotel; it reminded her of an old-fashioned wet room. She peeled off her now rough and stiff clothes.

After the long hot shower, she felt almost normal again, not realizing how filthy she had become. The makeup, hair spray, sweat, and blood created a morbid mask of the night. She wrapped herself in the fluffy towel and grabbed some clothes from her bag. Once dressed, she sat on the bed and put on her socks. A chill crept up her spine as her vision trailed. She rested her head in her hands while she waited for it to stop sloshing around like a dinghy in an angry sea. "What—the—fuck?" she whispered.

Once the lightheadedness subsided, she rummaged through her bag for a sweatshirt when she found the remaining dream root and Jonas's journal. Biting off a piece, she tossed the rest back into her bag, grabbed her jacket and slipped the journal into the inside pocket, her fingers lingering on the exposed edge. Exhaustion hit her like a wrecking ball. *Am I safe here?* She looked under the bed, then around the room for a makeshift weapon. *Just in case.* But there was nothing. *Well, I will be up every ten minutes, but I might as well try.* She pressed her back against the wall as she lay, her attention fixated on the door. The soft pillow cradled her head, not too firm, not too soft. She struggled to fight off sleep when she slid her hand under the pillow, then jerked it back.

Cautiously lifting it up, she found a knife; its unique steel handle had five identical holes running from its end to the black plastic sheath protecting the silver blade. The memory of Maya's lifeless corpse came back. She had killed her. She had killed a living being. A knot formed in her chest, still undecided if keeping the blade was sentimental or more twisted like a killer and their trophy. A folded piece of paper sat underneath it. *Until I return* was written in thin slanted letters. "How did you manage that one, Theo?" she whispered to the empty room. Repositioning the pillow, she wrapped her hand around the hilt of the knife underneath before falling asleep.

A LIGHT TAP on the door jolted her awake. She sat up, clutching the handle of the knife, frantically scanning for a threat. She recognized the room. She glanced at the silver blade as a fleck of ambient light danced across its edge. Taking several deep calming breaths, she returned the blade to its sheath under the pillow and ran her hand across her head. *I'm fine, I'm fine. Fucking asshole.* The tap sounded again.

"Kelly, are you awake? I have coffee," Autumn's voice sounded from outside the door. Kelly got up, flicked the lock, and jerked the handle; the door crept open as she returned to the bed, propping her head on her hands.

"How did you sleep?" Autumn stood in the doorway, a single white to-go cup in her hand. Kelly could feel her probing gaze on her.

"Okay, I guess," she answered. Focusing on the floor instead of Autumn, she grabbed the pair of boots she had missed earlier, slid them on, then grabbed her jacket.

"Come, we have things to take care of," Autumn said, handing Kelly the to-go cup.

They turned down the hall and headed to the atrium. Small groups were scattered about discussing political matters and recent events. Kelly studied the occupants' different auras emanating from each. The flashes of fangs and strange glares. She even spotted a small group with the same colored smoke dancing off their skin like Evalyn had back at Alexander's, but their smoke was different, lighter, with shades of yellow and gold.

"Autumn," a voice called from across the hall. An athletically built woman strode toward them in what appeared to be leather armor. Her long, golden, hair had been pulled back into a thick braid starting on top of her head and running down to the middle of her back. The dark, worn, vest she wore over a forest green tunic appeared rigid and thick unlike the leather leggings that moved with ease allowing them to be tucked into a pair of knee-high boots that matched the same rigid style. She had bodyguards on either side, both brawny and stoic, wearing similar attire to the woman. Kelly's eyes fell to the sheath hanging from the woman's hip. *Is that a sword?*

"Chancellor, how are you?" Autumn clasped her forearm, then pecked her on each cheek.

"I'd like to introduce Ms. Kelly Frost. Kelly, this is Hilda Helvig, High Chancellor for the Council of the Eternals," Autumn said. The Chancellor's attention turned to Kelly.

"So, *this* is Ms. Frost." She stared, intrigued, slowly circling and studying her. Kelly's skin prickled in apprehension as she stood squeezing the jacket. "Fascinating, absolutely fascinating," the chancellor muttered.

Kelly held out her hand once she stopped. Hilda clasped it similar to the way she had with Autumn. Hilda turned Kelly's arm, examined the mark and smirked.

"It's a pleasure to meet you." Hilda turned her attention back to Autumn. "The council requests your presence at today's meeting."

"Of course. I will get Kelly settled and head straight over." Autumn bowed her head.

Hilda jerked her head in a quick nod, glanced once more at Kelly, then headed off down the hallway. Kelly stood watching Hilda disappear into the crowd. *What was that all about?*

"Is she—" Kelly turned to speak to Autumn, but she was already halfway to the elevators. Kelly took off at a run to catch up to her.

"Where are we going?" Kelly asked, the metal gate rattling as Autumn pulled it closed. The elevator whined and groaned as it lifted them back to the lobby.

"You'll see," Autumn responded auspiciously.

"Was she carrying a sword?"

"She never goes anywhere without it."

"Why? Is she human?"

"In a sense. She is like Omari, Fiona, and me."

"A witch?"

"Witch is a more commonplace term. Do you remember what I told you about the Ancients?"

"Yeah, um…" Kelly's forehead wrinkled as she struggled to remember. "They were the first to harness the earth's hidden power. Some chose good, others not so much. They scattered until a time they could be safe and free."

"She is an ancient known as a Spá-kona. An Arch-Magi with the ability to sense the paths of some people."

"The paths?" Kelly asked.

"Instead of seeing, she feels the *aura* of your future. On occasion she gets a tangible fragment like an image, or a word, but those are special cases."

"What about you, Omari, and Fiona?"

"Omari and I are Arch-Magi; Fiona became a Magi the night you two met."

"What's the difference?"

"The level of training, children, or those just starting are known as Tenderfoots. Then they become savants, then apprentices. Once they become a Magi, they have completed their training unless their magic is inherited, then they can become an Arch-Magi and specialize in certain elements."

"Magi? Weren't those the three wise men that traveled to Bethlehem?"

"Magi began long before the birth of Christ. One of the downfalls of time is accuracy, but it can also be beneficial."

"How so?"

"Truth turns to rumor, then to story, then to legend and myth, until one day it ceases to exist at all. It made the world larger and easier to hide in." Kelly gave her a confused look. Autumn continued, "Modern inventions like mobile phones, dash cameras and video surveillance have made the human world smaller, more attainable. As a direct result, our kind is finding it harder to hide."

Kelly fell silent, her mind swimming with the new information. The metal gate creaked as Autumn pulled it open.

"Then how have you managed to stay hidden?"

They stepped out onto the street. Autumn stopped, turning Kelly toward her. She placed a hand over Kelly's eyes and whispered, "*Abditus*" then removed her hand. "Tell me what you see."

"An intersection in an alley."

"Try again, take your time and really look," Autumn said, moving behind her. Kelly scanned the beige exterior walls that lined either side of the narrow street. It was a street, nothing special, nothing different. She turned to face Autumn.

"An intersection in and *old* alley." Kelly shrugged, when over Autumn's shoulder the entrance to the council caught her eye. There was something off, something was missing.

Autumn covered Kelly's eyes again and whispered, "*Detego*."

"Once more."

Kelly's gaze flicked from Autumn's face back to the entrance. The council's symbol returned to the stone.

"Wha—? How?" she stumbled.

"There are things in this world that are only visible to supernatural creatures. The council's seal is one of them. Before the ritual, you had one foot in each world. Once it was performed, it pulled you completely into the supernatural world."

CHAPTER
SIX

K elly followed Autumn down the street. Tilting her head back, she soaked in the warmth of the midday sun as the new information swam in her head. They turned abruptly down a cobbled alley that stopped in front of a large brick building. The plain black door was overshadowed by a large bay window next to it filled with stacks of books and loose papers, leaving only a thin space at the top for the sun to shine in. She climbed the two small steps to the door when Autumn stopped and removed her buzzing phone from a hidden pocket in her dress

"I need to take this. Go ahead, I will be right in," she said, raising her phone and turning from the door, pressing her finger to her unoccupied ear.

Kelly stared at the door for a moment, hesitating. Her stomach tightened with anticipation, all her senses heightened. There was an energy emanating from the other side of this door. It pulled at her. There was something almost familiar about it. She turned the brass doorknob, pushed it open, and stepped inside. There was a narrow entryway with a staircase leading to the second floor. An opening to her left caught her eye; the door had been removed. She wandered into the room. A long table sat in the center, covered with odd-shaped beakers and vials, in a confusing yet intricate design. At the end of the setup, a glass beaker with blue liquid bubbled and smoked. Next to it was an old wooden box filled with dried flowers and other herbs, a mortar and pestle, and several books open to different pages and papers scattered about. Leaning, she read some of the more legible notes. Something clawed at the back of her mind. *Why does this look familiar?*

"Don't touch that. The kitchen is just there, the kettle is already on the stove. The tea leaves are in the cupboard, and you should be able to locate the milk without any difficulty. I will have it in my study." A slender, distinguished man in a tweed vest and slacks reached the bottom of the stairs and headed for the back of the house, never lifting his eyes from the book in his hand.

"Er..." Kelly glanced around, trying to figure out who he was talking to. She stepped out into the hall and glanced at the front door, then in the direction the man had gone. *Where did Autumn go? Who is this guy?* Kelly wandered down the hall, spotting the kitchen and continued into the room the man had entered.

He sat in a large leather chair behind an ornate oak desk in the center of the room. The walls were covered in floor-to-ceiling bookshelves filled with leather-bound books; the only space not covered was a pair of French doors behind the desk and a fireplace on the far end. Every inch of the desktop was covered in papers and open books. The man was hunched over several books, jotting notes on a scrap of paper.

"Just set it on the desk and you can begin cleaning the

lab. Be sure to use extreme caution as there are plenty of volatile items and we don't need the place burning down." His tone, brisk and apathetic. His gaze flitted to the only clear spot, then returned to his papers. An uncomfortable silence fell between them.

"What part did you not understand?" he said, looking up from his stack of books, utter annoyance engraved on his face.

"Sorry but..." Kelly stammered.

"American. Bloody hell." He pushed up his horn-rimmed glasses and pinched at the bridge of his nose.

"What's that supposed to mean?" Kelly snarled.

"Oh, wonderful. You have met," Autumn said delightedly, entering the room.

"This is who the council has sent? She's an American. Does she even know how to clean properly? I imagine she can't even make a decent cup of tea. Tell the council if they want me to figure out what is going on, then I need someone with a modicum of competence."

"Wow, fuck you, Ebenezer," Kelly snapped.

"No, Jo-Jo, she's not your housekeeper."

"Thank God for that. I have told you a hundred times, Ms. Kazem, don't call me Jo-Jo."

"Kelly Frost, let me introduce you to Jonas Wainwright."

"Wainwright?" Kelly echoed. As if by reflex she pressed the hidden journal in her jacket against her side, all the air in her lungs vanished. "You're... you're," she stuttered, trying to turn the memory of the journal's pages and the images she had created into coherent thought.

"Yes, profes—" Jonas boasted, straightening in his chair.

"You're my ancestor," Kelly cut him off. He looked up at

her over the rim of his glasses. His stormy blue eyes were like looking in a mirror.

"Don't be ridiculous," he scoffed.

"A man sees the wickedness in the world and takes note so that he may snuff it out," she recited.

"Where did you hear that?" He stiffened, his eyes locked on to hers. *Touched a nerve?*

"I didn't hear it, I read it. Your father said it to you on your birthday when he gave you this." She pulled the journal out of her pocket. He sprang from his chair and snatched it from her hand, then thumbed through the pages. A sentimental look flicked across his face.

"I will let you two get further acquainted. I must attend to some council business. Jo-Jo, play nice," Autumn said, then left the room.

"Where did you get this? Did you steal it?"

"No, I didn't steal it. I got it from my mother," she said through gritted teeth.

Jonas removed his glasses, pinching the bridge of his nose and let out a deep sigh. Clasping his hands behind his back, he circled Kelly twice, then leaned against his desk, crossing his arms.

"Do you have any siblings? A brother perhaps?"

"No, I'm an only child." Silence fell as Jonas continued to study her.

"Why am I here?"

"What have you been told?"

"Jack shit," she seethed, trying to not let his rudeness get the better of her. "Maybe you have the answers I am looking for."

"Why would I have answers for you?" His condescending tone dug at her.

"You're my great, great, great grandfather."

"Your point?"

"According to that journal, we have shared similar... side effects." Her annoyance flared as she wrestled with the urge to keep her business and the events of the past few weeks to herself. She took a deep, steadying breath. "I was in an accident a couple years ago and ever since I had these headaches, which would range from minor inconvenience to blinding agony."

The hardened expression on his face shifted from agitation to intrigue. Kelly continued.

"Then I met Autumn and her friends, and she said there was a possible cure. I went through this strange ritual, then I was kidnapped by a vampire named Alexander. He had me imprisoned and tortured for a week, I guess. It felt like a lifetime. Autumn and her friends came to save me and—" She paused, trying to explain what exactly happened without sounding even more insane. "My cell door, er, blew off its hinges."

Jonas sat, his brows furrowed, combing over what she had told him.

"What do you mean 'blew off'?"

"Like a bomb. The door was on the frame. There was a metal crunching sound, then it was ten feet down the hall and bent like a piece of tinfoil."

"Impossible!"

"Says the man that's been living for almost two centuries."

"We need to run some tests," he mumbled, brushing past her, heading for the front door.

"Would you like to share with the class, professor?" she taunted.

He stopped at the coat rack by the door, shrugged on a

matching tweed jacket with leather elbow patches, grabbed his hat, and bounded out the door.

"Keep up," he called over his shoulder. Kelly jogged to catch up with him, then easily kept in stride as they made their way back to the council's entrance. *Quick for an old guy.*

They waited in an uncomfortable silence for the elevator.

"Why don't they have stairs? It would be faster," she commented, trying to ease the uncomfortable silence.

"If you don't have anything positive to say, don't say anything at all. No one wants to hear you complain."

"I'm *positive* this is the slowest elevator in the world," she satirized. He glared at her from the corner of his eye. The elevator clunked to a stop before them.

CHAPTER
SEVEN

Jonas bustled down the hall to an office at the end. He pushed open the door as if owning the place, sending a burst of antiseptic air around them. Even though she was used to it, the smell still made her gag. The room was a surprisingly typical examination room with plain off-white walls, a small examination table, a cupboard with a sink, and a cabinet. Jonas picked up a clipboard off the counter next to the sink and jotted some notes. He turned around to see Kelly standing in the doorway.

"Well, go on, sit down."

"Um no, you haven't told me shit. Why am I here?"

"My god, child, how slow are you? We are here for tests."

"I meant here in Versailles. I'm going to ignore the fact we are related for a moment. Where's your medical license? Are you even qualified to examine someone?"

A sharp prickle filled her nose; unable to fight it, she sneezed.

"May I help you? Ah, Professor Wainwright, I didn't expect to see you today."

Kelly whirled around. A slender man stood in the doorway. Although he was average height, she was slightly taller. His freshly buzzed jet-black hair and clean-shaven face highlighted his angular cheekbones and chiseled jaw. His flawless bronze skin glowing against his dark brown eyes.

"Will?" her every muscle tensed.

"Call me Billy. Kelly, is that really you? How are you?" He beamed.

"What are you doing here?" she snarled.

"How do you know this woman?" Jonas asked.

"Oh, we go way back." Billy winked in Kelly's direction.

"He's my ex-boyfriend," she clarified through gritted teeth.

"Still angry?"

"Still keeping secrets?" she snapped.

"Doctor Dakota, I need a full workup, physical, blood work, ECG, CAT, everything," Jonas ordered, flipping through the pages on the clipboard while jotting notes.

"Anything specific I should be looking for?"

Jonas glanced at Kelly, then Billy. "I need the results as soon as possible. You know where to find me. Don't let her out of your sight." Jonas left the room, disappearing down the hall.

"You know?" she asked.

"Know?" he echoed innocently.

"Magic, vampires, all *this* shit." She waved her hands.

"Oh, yeah."

"How long?" she asked. Billy fell silent. "How long? Straight answer." Her new aggravation becoming clouded with the memories of their history.

"Long enough," he sighed.

"And you're okay with it? It doesn't freak you out?"

"No, shall we get started?" He gestured to the examination table.

"I don't think so." She crossed her arms and leaned against the wall.

"Come on, Kelly, I am a professional. It's nothing I haven't seen before."

Her lip twitched reflexively in a snarl. *What if this is how I get my answers, how I find out what is going on?*

"At least tell me you have a nurse or something," Kelly said, letting out a reluctant sigh.

"You are safe here."

"It's not for my safety, it's for yours."

Billy pressed a button on the wall that resembled an old-fashioned doorbell, then grabbed the blood pressure cuff, O2 reader, and thermometer from the cabinet.

"How have you been?"

"Fine."

"When did you get out?" he asked, wrapping the cuff around her bicep. Kelly sneezed again. "Bless you." He handed her a tissue.

"Almost a year ago. You still have that damn cat?" she snarled. A smirk flicked across his lips as he watched the gauge. After a moment, he released the pressure and with the loud rip of Velcro removed the cuff and jotted down some numbers.

"I heard about Eric. I'm sorry for your loss." His voice softened along with his expression. He slid the thermometer across her forehead.

"Which time?"

"Both actually. I'm sorry I couldn't make it to the funeral." His brow furrowed as he copied the number.

"You had your orders. It was all just a waste, anyway." Her voice became just as cold and void of emotion as it had been that day. "Wait, what happened to your orders?"

"Nothing. They weren't orders, they were my discharge papers. I was offered a job here, so I took it. Are you experiencing any fever? Cold chills? Dizziness?"

A light tap sounded on the door. A petite woman in powder blue scrubs came in pushing a crash cart. On top sat a tray with some empty vials, packaged needles, and swabs.

"She's going to take some blood and do a quick ECG."

"Good, you suck with a needle. You're not a vampire, right?" she asked, turning to the nurse.

"No, I am human, became an apprentice a year ago, actually."

"Once she gets what she needs, we are going to head down the hall for the scans and the athletics stress test," Billy noted as he flipped through Jonas's notes. Kelly looked at him, confused.

"It's not your standard physical," he said with a coy smile before exiting the exam room, closing the door behind him.

The woman worked quickly, tightening the rubber tourniquet, swabbing the site and sticking her with the needle before Kelly had time to bat an eye. Her expression contorted with silent questions as the blood filled the vials at an almost alarming rate. The woman removed the needle and replaced it with a bandage.

"I need to apply these leads; can you remove your shirt please?" the woman asked tenderly. Kelly did as she said and sat as the nurse fiddled away with the machine and jotted more notes. Kelly's mind wandered. *Jonas Wain-*

wright is alive. What's that expression? Don't meet your heroes. We can't be related. How is he so narrow-minded?

"All done. You can get redressed," the nurse chimed, just as her thoughts overlapped. She gave Kelly a genuine smile and turned to pile her supplies onto the tray while Kelly pulled her shirt back on, then glided out of the room.

Billy stood outside the open door, gesturing for Kelly to follow him. They made their way down the hall, coming to a stop at a set of double doors. He pushed through one side into a small breezeway.

"First, we are going to take a few scans. Locker room is through there." He pointed at a door on the left. "There should be a set of clothes for you. Once you have changed, I'll meet you through those doors." He pointed to the door next to the locker room.

"Why are we taking scans?"

He flipped, jotting more notes on the clipboard.

"Hello, are you going to answer me?" she growled.

"I don't know. Professor Wainwright wants them, so he gets them. Please change. We have a lot to do," he said, looking up. She huffed and pushed her way into the locker room.

The set of clothes left made her recoil, fighting back the urge to vomit, a once white men's tank top was stained brownish-yellow and folded neatly on a pair of navy-blue shorts, that she assumed were as old as the shirt. She spun on her heel and went back through the door.

Billy was adjusting the computer table when he glanced out the door at her. "You didn't change."

"Nope, those clothes should be set on fire. I am pretty sure they are from the '50s or something. It's also quite possible something is living in them."

"The machine is going to pick up any metal. Your

clothes will interfere with that, and I need to put you through a series of athletic stress tests. You will need a full range of motion."

"I'm fine."

"You can't run in boots and jeans."

"You know perfectly well I can." Kelly cocked an eyebrow, remembering the many times their unit had to run endless miles in their uniforms.

"Give me a minute," he huffed, pulling a cell phone out of his pocket and walking out of earshot. After a moment, he returned.

"Someone is getting you a different set of clothes. In the meantime, change into this for the scan," he said, shrugging off his white lab coat and handing it to her.

She reluctantly took his lab coat and sneezed, then went to change. Besides the occasional direction from Billy, neither said a word to the other. The intermittent clack of the machine marking the time like a broken clock. Once he was done, she returned to the locker room and changed back into her clothes. She zipped the front of her leather jacket and dug her hands deep into its pockets, pushing her way out of the locker room and through the door directly across the breezeway.

The room was somewhere between an old high school gymnasium and a storage closet with equipment scattered about. There was a treadmill, punching bag, pull-up bars, and a few other items she had only seen in the Olympics or movies set in the '50s and '60s. Billy was next to the treadmill, connecting it to a laptop with a set of long leads. Kelly walked over and examined the treadmill; it was relatively new, unlike most of the other equipment. She tossed the lab coat to him.

"We will start with strength." He began jotting notes as

they walked over to the punching bag. "Stay here," he told her, several feet away from the bag. She looked up to see the bag was mounted onto a rail. He slipped behind the bag and pushed; it glided forward. Billy stopped the bag a few feet away from her, then checked the side of the rail, jotted a few notes and stepped back. "First, I need you to punch the bag with half effort."

"Why?" she asked, folding her arms across her chest.

"It's part of the test."

"I got that part. Why am I being tested?"

"You will have to ask Professor Wainwright."

"I'm asking you."

"I told you I don't know, and I won't know until the tests are complete. In my experience, it's better to have all the information before forming a theory. Jonas, on the other hand, is the opposite and wouldn't request all of this if he didn't have a suspicion or two. Now please punch the bag."

Kelly stayed rooted to the spot.

"This would go smoother if you didn't question every detail. Do I have to make it an order?"

"You can, but it won't change anything. I'm not your subordinate."

She squared herself up to the bag and punched it, using half her effort; the bag glided back a little way. Billy looked up to the side of the rail, jotted some notes, then pushed the bag back to the starting point.

"This time, use all your strength."

Kelly let out an annoyed sigh, removed her jacket, and squared up again. She stared at the plain black leather, her mind drifting, grasping at the thousand questions that were still not being answered. Heat rose in her chest. She made a fist and threw another punch as hard as she could.

The bag hurtled back, slamming to a stop against the wall. Billy stared at the side of the rail, then at Kelly, failing to hide his look of shock. Her anger dampened her own surprise. She knew even the strongest person on earth couldn't move a heavy bag that far. She gritted her teeth. *What is happening to me?*

Billy returned to his clipboard, his pen scribbling across the paper.

"What are you writing?" Kelly growled.

"Only numbers at the moment, they should make sense later," he said as the petite nurse that had taken Kelly's blood made her way across the gym with a manila folder and a shopping bag. She handed the folder to Billy and the bag to Kelly, then left.

"Go change, then we can do the treadmill test."

"What do the numbers mean?"

"Kelly, we need to finish the tests. Please go change." His tone became more annoyed.

Kelly bit back her retort, headed back to the locker room and changed into her new clothes: a black and white tracksuit and sneakers. Making sure her laces were snug, she sat up. Her vision blurred as the now familiar sensation of her brain sloshing against her skull raged again. After a few deep breaths, it faded and her vision returned. *What the fuck.* When she returned to the gym, Billy was back at the treadmill, tapping away at the laptop's keyboard.

"We are going to start with a light jog to get your heart rate up."

Kelly removed the track jacket and climbed onto the treadmill. Billy applied the leads to several places on her chest and stomach, wrapped a blood pressure cuff around her bicep, and pushed the start button. The belt crawled into motion; Kelly's walk turned into a shuffle, then a jog as she hammered the increase speed button.

"How long?" she asked, locking her gaze on the far wall.

"Shall we say... ten minutes?"

Kelly's mind drifted, all the aggravation and questions slipping away. She pictured Eric running with her like they used to. Then his image changed, his auburn hair darkening and growing longer as his torso stretched and expanded. He turned his head. Theo was now with her. Her heart swelled. She pictured the woods back home, the river, the clearing. What she would give to be back there right now when everything had seemed to disappear.

"That's time," Billy said, snapping her out of her trance. He pressed the slow button until she came to a stop. He handed her a water and read the screen. "How do you feel?"

"Fine," she shrugged.

"We will give it about two minutes, then increase the speed."

Kelly nodded distractedly. She wasn't panting, her heart was just as steady as before she ran, even though heat radiated through her she hadn't broken a sweat.

"Where was your head when you were running?" Billy asked.

"None of your business."

"Kelly. You can still talk to me."

"Home, okay? There's no better place to escape everything than the woods back home."

"Still do a lot of running?"

"It's the only thing that quiets my mind."

"Then why do you look more agitated than when you started?"

"A lot happened and all I'm getting is more questions than answers."

"Ready to go again?" he asked. She scowled. "What? Not funny?"

She set the untouched water and pressed the start button once again. Hammering the increase speed button until she was sprinting. Her mind drifted again, faster this time. As her memory merged with imagination, the room around her dissolved. Theo was in front of her as they bobbed and weaved through the forest back home.

"Time." Billy's voice shattered her trance once again.

Kelly pressed the button, slowing to a stop, her heart rate only slightly elevated. Billy tapped a few keys on the laptop, then began removing the blood pressure cuff and leads from her.

"Okay, I have all the information I need. Go ahead and change, and I'll bring you back to Professor Wainwright."

"I know the way. I don't need an escort."

"It is not about whether you know the way or not, it's about your safety."

"Safety? Alexander is dead. I am safe."

"Go change please." He sighed.

EIGHT

As they entered Jonas's study, he was once again hidden behind his desk obscured by more books that had been added in her absence. Kelly spotted a chair in the corner hiding under yet another stack of books. She moved them onto the small table next to it, then dragged the chair over to Jonas's desk and sat. Billy handed him the folder containing her test results. His stoic features faltered, letting out a glimmer of astonishment for a fraction of a moment before regaining his composure and knitting his brow.

"Impossible! Is this right?" Jonas asked in disbelief.

"Saw it with my own eyes," Billy answered, a bit smugly.

"When you were experiencing your headaches, how long did you sleep each night?" Jonas directed the question to Kelly, picking up a pen with his eyes still on the file.

"I don't know, between four and six hours." She shrugged.

"And now?"

"Two hours tops."

"Were they consistent? Time, location, intensity?"

"No, they were often worse when I went into the city." She paused, remembering the night she first met Theo and Eli. "There were a couple times it nearly blinded me."

His eyes flitted to her, then Billy, then back to the file as he scratched notes.

"Healthy diet?"

"What does that matter? Do you even know what's going on?" she scoffed. Jonas glanced at her, his cold eyes penetrating her moody exterior much like her father's had done so many times when she was younger. She caught Billy out of the corner of her eye. He flashed her a look she knew all too well. *Stop arguing and just answer the question.*

"I guess."

"It's simply impossible," Jonas repeated. Dropping the pen onto the open file, he leaned back in his chair, pressing his fingers together against his lips.

"Obviously not," Kelly grunted. "Are you going to tell what the fuck is wrong with me? Why I just did this shit?"

Jonas was taken aback. "Does your husband know you use such language?"

"Husband, ha," Kelly scoffed. Out of the corner of her eye, Billy scratched his nose in a poor attempt to cover his smile. She thought of Theo. It had only been a couple of weeks and they had never put a label on whatever they had. *It's too new, and yet...* An unsettledness surged in her chest. "I'm not married."

"I have to get back; you know where to find me if you need me," Billy said, glancing at his watch and leaving the room. As the front door quietly clicked shut, the overwhelming silence of old-fashioned values clashing with the modern world suffocated the room. A sanctimonious expression rooted itself on Jonas's face.

"So, what do the results say?" Kelly asked. Jonas sat up and shuffled through the stacks of papers and books, scanning the weathered pages.

"The symptoms are similar... but," he muttered, more to himself.

"Similar? Similar to what? Do you know what's happening to me?"

The question lingered in the silence; his focus locked on the page in front of him. She obnoxiously cleared her throat.

"I do not have the time or patience to put it in terms you would understand."

Her jaw clenched so tightly a sharp pain shot through her teeth. Any harder, and she would crack a tooth.

"Just tell me," she demanded, her voice shaking as she struggled to hold back her temper.

"We will revisit it tomorrow," he said, pulling a pocket watch from his vest. "I must prepare for tomorrow's trial. I assume you can manage your way back to your room." He closed the file, setting it off to the side and returned to his work.

"Why can't you tell me now?"

"Because I have more important things to do at this present moment."

"What am I supposed to do until then?"

"I am sure you can find something to occupy your time. There must be something to bake or knit in the meantime."

"Or you can tell me now because I am not some dimwitted housewife you are accustomed to," she snapped, her anger bubbling over.

"My word is final, and you would do right to abide by it."

A light tap sounded behind her. Kelly whipped around

to see a large, bald, bronze-skinned man standing in the doorway.

"Are you ready to go? There is someone that wishes to see you," Omari said in his deep, ominous groan that had once terrified but now comforted her.

CHAPTER
NINE

Kelly followed Omari through the atrium down the clinic hallway and into the stairwell at the end. After descending one flight, they stepped into a partially darkened hall. The floor they entered stopped short. A few feet in front of them was a wall with a single door and a guard perched on a stool to one side.

"Good evening, Valgard, I'd like to see her," Omari said to the guard. The guard got up from his stool and towered over them. The sides of his head had been shaved and the remaining long golden hair was pulled into a thick braid of smaller twists and braids held together with leather cordage. His loose linen shirt and denim pants hid his battle-hardened body. A long leather belt wrapped around his waist with his sword ready if needed.

"Who is this?" Valgard cocked an eyebrow in Kelly's direction.

"A friend," Omari smiled.

"The Council authorization?"

"Right here," he said, handing Valgard a slip of paper. He read it, then nodded, then handed it back to Omari.

"You only have fifteen minutes till the evening meal, then lights out."

"Not a problem, thank you."

Valgard opened the door, Omari and Kelly slipped inside. The remainder of the hall on the other side reminded her of the cells she and the others had been kept in at Alexander's mansion—depressing walls broken only by cell doors. They passed several doors on either side before Omari stopped. The iron bars of the cell door formed a weight in her stomach. On the other side was the small, fiery redhead lying on a cot and reading.

"How are you holding up?" Kelly asked, her guilt catching in her throat. Fiona looked up from her book, her face brightening. She tossed it on the cot and bolted to the door. Fiona seemed to do alright. Her normally free-flowing hair had been pulled into a loose braid. Though her face was bright and full of life, the bags under her eyes felt wrong.

"Kelly! How are you? What are you doing here? You should be in London with Theo having a relaxing holiday. Oh no, did something happen? What did he do? What's going on? You have to tell me everything." Kelly could barely make out the questions as they flew from Fiona at supersonic speed.

"I'm good," she chuckled, "we got word about your trial."

"But why are you here? Autumn would have sent word once we had an outcome. You didn't have to ruin your—" Fiona cleared her throat "—personal time."

"After all you did for me, do you really think I would stay in London and not be here to support and fight for you?"

Fiona grinned broadly at Kelly. It was obvious how

much her coming to visit meant to Fiona. They both slunk to the floor. Kelly told her about London and meeting Wyatt and the awkward run-in with Gabriella. Kelly's smile faltered, the weight in her stomach becoming heavier with every smile and childlike laugh from Fiona. Kelly broke her gaze away from the innocent face across from her and landed on the bars between them. There were sharp, runic symbols carved along the base of the door and the inside of the frame.

"What's wrong?" Fiona asked, tilting her head. Kelly pulled her knees to her chest, loosely wrapping her arms around them.

"It's my fault you're in here."

"No, it's not. It was my choice; I knew the consequences and to our family... to me, your life and safety are worth more than any punishment the council issues."

"It's really not."

"Do we really have to do this again? You are special, more special than you realize."

"Top secret special," Kelly huffed.

"What do you mean?"

"My self-righteous ancestor Jonas and Doctor Dakota made me do some bizarre tests and now they won't tell me what it all means and what is happening to me."

"I like Billy, he's nice." Kelly shot her a look. "You don't like him?"

"He's my ex." Her body became unnaturally stiff as she tried to fight the memories.

Silence fell between them. The pained expression that deformed Fiona's naïve face gnawed at Kelly's insides. Fiona opened and closed her mouth a few times before breaking the silence.

"What does Theo say about the test results?"

"I haven't seen him since we got here. He said he had to see Fabian, but—"

"I am sorry, my dear, but it is time for us to go. We will see you in the morning," Omari interrupted. They both got to their feet. Fiona held up her hand, stopped only by the magical barricade. Kelly copied her.

"Don't worry, everything will be fine. You'll be out in no time," she said, smiling at Fiona's round childlike face through the bars. Omari and Kelly headed back toward the entrance when a voice caught her attention.

"You really think the council is just going to let her illegal dreamwalking slide? I don't think so," a disheveled Evalyn called from the far end of her cell. She was in the same outfit she had been in the last time Kelly saw her. Only now it was riddled with tears and loose pieces of fabric. Her hair sticking up in several places and her once perfect makeup, now smudged and faded.

"What are you doing here, Evalyn?" Kelly growled.

"Not very bright, are you? I have been arrested. Idiot," she said.

"Tends to happen when you break the law."

"What do you know about our laws, you petulant child?"

"She broke the law to save a life. What did you do it for? Money? Power?"

"You shouldn't talk of things you do not know," Evalyn snarled.

"We must go," Omari said, nudging Kelly's side. She shot one last glare at Evalyn, then the two started back toward the door. Still several feet away, the door opened and the blonde woman from Delirium strode past them.

Ga... Gabriella? Her periwinkle pantsuit hugged her figure. An overpowering cloud of *Chanel No. 5* saturated the air as she passed. *What is she doing here?* Kelly glanced over her shoulder, watching as Gabriella stopped at Evalyn's cell. Kelly slowed to a crawl, trying to eavesdrop on their conversation.

"Why are you here?" Evalyn snarled.

"As a reminder." Gabriella's hushed tone had an air of assertiveness to it. An unexpected contrast to the way she sounded at Delirium.

"I don't need a reminder; I know what is at stake," Evalyn snapped.

"Then keep your mouth shut or King Trevan will find out what you have really been up to."

Omari pulled Kelly's elbow through the door. They left the cell wing and crossed the Atrium toward her room.

"When is the trial?"

"Tomorrow, eleven o'clock."

"Eleven? Why so late?"

"Evalyn's sentencing is first."

"When was her trial?"

"This morning."

"Oh. Who is King Trevan?"

They reached her room. Omari paused, looking pensively at a spot on Kelly's door.

"Someone you don't need to worry about. Get some rest. We will come and get you when it's time."

"I'll try, oh have you seen Theo? I haven't heard from him since we got here."

"No, but if I see him, I will let him know. Good night."

"Night." Kelly fought her best to smile genuinely, even though her chest and mind were heavy with anticipation

72

and now new questions. If only she could guarantee Fiona's outcome.

She plopped on her bed, staring up at the plain ceiling. Sliding the blade and the note from Theo out from under her pillow, she lingered over his elegant penmanship, then unsheathed the blade and fiddled with it, balancing it between her index fingers on each hand.

CHAPTER
TEN

How long had she been staring into the dark void above her? An hour? Two? Lying there, one hand under her head, the other gripped loosely around the hilt of the knife on her stomach. The barrage of unanswered questions growing and repeating in a never-ending cycle. They were just white noise now, a constant buzzing in her mind making her muscles twitch with heightened awareness and the need for action. With a heavy sigh, she sat up, placing her bare feet on the cold tile floor.

Her cheeks grew uncomfortably hot, and the room spun again. *Fuck, I need to cool down.* As she stood, the room spun more violently, sending her crashing to the floor. "God damn it!" she grunted, her hands and knees stinging from the sudden impact. She crawled the remaining distance to the bathroom.

Once she reached the sink, she gripped the edge of the basin, closed her eyes and hoisted herself back onto her feet. Blindly turning the tap, she let the water run for a moment before splashing her face. The cold water sent a chill down her spine, signaling future relief while adding to her concern. She took a couple of slow deep breaths, letting the water take effect before opening her eyes. Though the room had stopped spinning, her insides squirmed and twisted, sending sharp cramps through her stomach and chest. She tried to take another deep breath but was cut short as the contents of her stomach forced their way out. She gripped the base of the tap for support as her stomach twisted in breathtaking pain. Tears crept from her eyes. *What the fuck is going on?* She heaved and then stared, stunned, at the basin.

The white porcelain was speckled with red, strains of blood mixed with the water as it rinsed away. She glanced at her reflection; the red-tinted saliva clung to her bottom lip. "What the fuck?" she whispered, leaning closer to the mirror, prodding her lip with her finger. Her subconscious took over, cleaning the basin and rinsing her mouth several times before examining her mouth. *That was too much to come from my gums. I didn't ingest any. Did I?* Her memories raced by as she sifted through, trying to remember when or how that much blood got into her stomach. "Nothing, no possible way." She glanced at her reflection again. "I need to tell Autumn." *It's late, I will tell her first thing.* She returned to her bed. Unable to sleep, she waited.

Becoming more restless as time ticked on. She listened as the footsteps in the hall died out. The occasional straggler passed by after a long silence. A low rumble followed by sloshing and a wet slap. The caretaker squelched the soapy water across the hall. Kelly focused. *He's on the far end.* It would be some time before it was quiet again. She focused on the rhythmic sound, hoping it would lull her to sleep. Instead, the repetitive slosh, slap, squelch set her teeth on edge.

Sitting up, she slid on her sneakers and tucked the knife into the bottom of her bag. Her knuckles hit something hard. Swapping it for the knife, she pulled out her phone. *How did I forget I had a phone? Not the first time, I guess.* She powered it on. The screen lit up, displaying seven laughing faces are frozen in the perfect moment. Fiona's birthday. Kelly's chest swelled as she thought back to that night. The moment of pure happiness. The freedom she felt as she and Theo barreled down the abandoned back road. Her eyes landed on Eric, though his face was as perfect as it had ever been, her mind twisted it, showing the devious intent underneath. The happiness suddenly replaced with the conflicting swirl of betrayal and forgiveness. *He didn't have control; it wasn't his fault.* Even though she knew it was true, the thoughts of Eric's actions still pained her.

Breaking away from the photo, she glanced at the symbols in the corner. *2:15 a.m. Battery, over half. No Wi-Fi. No service.* She held her phone up automatically. Nothing. *Who am I going to call at 2 a.m. anyway? Eli? Mom and Dad? I don't know what time it is there. What would I even say? "Hey, Mom, so vampires and magic are real, and I met Dad's ancestor Jonas, and I just threw up blood. What do I do?" Yeah right. Can't call Theo, he doesn't have a cell phone.* She let out an exasperated sigh. The slosh, slap, squelch became more irritating.

"Fuck this," she breathed, tucking the phone into her pocket and reaching for the door. Opening it just enough to see out, she glanced down the dimly lit hall in both directions. The caretaker was still at the end of the hall, hunched over his mop, his back to her. She slunk out into the hall and headed toward the atrium. She didn't have a plan or destination, but she knew staying in that small room would drive her insane.

The atrium had a strange energy, not like being the only person in a usually bustling area, but more like there were people still here only out of sight. Moseying around, she peeked down a couple of different darkened halls, each identical to the one before.

She stopped halfway across the next hall. Barely visible, she made out a pair of double doors. Making sure she was still alone, she headed for them. Carefully, she pushed the door open. There was a faint click followed by the room becoming brighter. *Really, motion sensor lights. So much for being stealthy here.*

She wandered over to the treadmill. *I'm a decent runner, but that test was easy, too easy. Why wasn't I tired, breathing heavy, even remotely sweating?* She inspected it, the walking belt, handrails, console, all standard factory parts. She tried prying at the plastic edge of the console. *Maybe they messed with the circuit panel inside.* There was a small crunch as the plastic case refused to cooperate. *Better not break it.* Annoyed at the lack of evidence of tampering, she abandoned the treadmill and resumed wandering.

Treating the contents of the gym like museum pieces. She paused in front of the neat pile of equipment that had been pushed against the wall for storage. There were uneven bars, parallel bars, a set of rings attached to long straps, and two pieces that she recognized from watching the Olympics.

After a few moments, she continued over to the punching bag. Still against the wall. *Maybe that punch was a fluke. They only had me do it once.* Kelly pushed the bag back to the opposite end of the rail. She rolled her shoulders and swung her arms, warming up her muscles, then squared up to the bag. Theo's instructions echoed in her mind. *Start at your shoulder, then turn your fist when you fully extend.* The bag glided back and came to a gradual stop a few inches back. *A fluke, I knew it.* Staring up at the marks on the side of the rail, her jaw tightened as a determination rooted itself in the back of her mind. *If I did it once, I can do it again.* She returned to the front of the bag. Taking a few deep breaths, she let her mind slip back to the forest with Theo, the ghost of his warm touch on her skin as he corrected her form. She took another deep breath, then punched. The bag glided back a few inches farther. A low growl escaped her chest. She returned the bag to the end. *I just want answers. What is happening? Why was I fucking kidnapped?* White-hot anger flooded her body as flashes of the pain, Alexander, the small cell and Theo chained to the floor in silver raced through her mind. She let out a guttural grunt as her fist slammed into the bag again. The bag hurtled back, followed by a muted thump as it hit the wall. She stood frozen in shock.

A faint hiss broke the silence. Slowly, she approached the bag. A small yet steady stream of sand poured from its seam. She reached out, letting it trickle across her hand before falling to the growing pile below. *Must be old stitching, that's all.* Her fingers danced along the seam from one stitch to the next. Besides the few that had broken, the stitches all appeared new, even reinforced.

A loud metal clunk echoed from the hall. She whipped her head around. *Fuck. I really don't want to explain this or why I'm alone.* As quietly as she could, she darted across the room to the door. Pressing her body to the wall, she steadied her breathing. *How long do I have to be still before the light goes out?* She listened intently as the footsteps grew louder. Sucking in a deep breath, she waited to be discovered when the lights clicked off and the room was filled with darkness. *Thank God*. She watched through the window in the door as three figures passed, uninterested.

"Right or left?" one voice asked in a loud whisper.

"Shut up," the second voice scolded in a hushed voice.

"Follow me," whispered the third.

Kelly slipped off her shoes and waited until the footsteps had mostly died before slipping into the hall. She crept to the end just in time to see the three figures turn down a different hall. Taking off at a quicker pace, she peeked her head around the corner.

"Are you sure this is right? It doesn't look right," the first voice said.

The second figure slammed the first into the wall. A glint of ambient light caught on the blade as he pushed it against the other's throat.

"Are you trying to get us caught?"

"N-No," the first figure stammered.

"Then shut the fuck up, or I'll do it for you by removing your tongue. You are only here as a courtesy. Let's get this done. Silently."

The first figure's silhouette nodded vigorously. The second figure returned the blade to its holster.

There was a crash followed by the splash of water on tile. A light in the distance flicked on.

Kelly snapped her head around, pressing herself against the wall.

"Come on, we have to hurry. Someone may have heard you," the third figure said. Kelly peeked around the corner in time to see the second figure's familiar black ponytail and the third's profile before they disappeared behind the door to the stairwell.

That can't be right.

The roar of the plastic wheel on tile grew louder. Kelly tore off across the atrium and down the hall, tucking into her room. She dropped her shoes on the floor, then plopped onto her bed.

What is he doing? Was that really... Zeke?

CHAPTER
ELEVEN

K elly jerked awake, gripping the hilt of the dagger on her chest. She held her breath, scanning the room before what woke her sounded again. Someone was at her door. Her dagger at the ready, she cracked it open. Theo stood before her holding two Styrofoam cups. Kelly relaxed, letting out a subconscious sigh, and swung the door fully open.

"Good morning, beautiful. How did you sleep?" he asked.

"As to be expected, I guess," she said, slumping back on her bed and rubbing her face. She glanced up at Theo, still standing outside the doorway. "What are you doing?"

"You have to invite me."

"I'm sorry, what?"

"Your room has protective enchantments around it."

"Oh, er, okay. Come in."

He stepped in and handed her a cup, then closed the door behind him.

"Thank you for the dagger. It helps, kind of. Where have you been? So much has been happening." She got up from her spot and walked over to the bathroom. "What time is it?" Turning on the faucet, she let the water run for a moment before splashing it on her face, the bags under her eyes a harsh reminder that something was wrong. *I need to tell him.*

"6:58 a.m."

"Shit," she breathed. "We gotta go." She pulled her hair back, bounding out of the bathroom.

"Fiona's trial is not till eleven. What is the rush?"

"Evelyn's here. She's being sentenced this morning." Theo opened the door for her. She stopped, looking up into his eyes. That comfort only he could give swelled in her chest, but something else was there, a dark weight. "What's wrong?"

"It can wait. I will tell you later," he said, trying to reassure her.

"Okay, I need to talk to you, too." She let out a reluctant sigh, and they both headed down the hall. Passing into the atrium, Theo led the way to a set of large wooden double doors. She eased open one side just enough for them to slip in unnoticed. Kelly paused for a moment, expecting to see a normal courtroom with a wall of wood paneling behind the large commanding wooden bench where the judge sat and two podiums for the involved parties, even a matching barricade in front of the gallery. Instead, they were at the top of a long staircase with rows of seats to either side wrapping around the room, making the floor at the bottom seem much smaller than it was. In the center was Evalyn, standing on a dais, her head bowed to the five red-robed figures sitting at a curved judge's bench. A thin sapphire blue aura surrounded her. The large theater was mostly empty, with a few spectators scattered through the stands.

Kelly found the nearest empty seats. Her eyes locked on

the proceedings below. She perched on the edge of her seat, leaning forward.

The red robe in the center stood, removing their cowl. The silence grew tense as Hilda glanced around the room. "Council member Rowan, could you remind those in attendance of the charges against Evalyn Gemfell?"

The red robe at the end of the bench stood. His strong features made the inscrutable expression across his face almost frightening. The deep timbre of his voice filled the room. A chill ran down her spine.

"The charges are aiding a known heretic of the council, torture, and using blood magic." Once he finished, he returned to his seat.

"Blood magic?" Kelly mouthed to Theo.

He rested his arm on the back of her seat and leaned in to whisper, "I will explain later." His warm breath caressed the side of her cheek. A wave of heat flooded her face. Her mind flashed through all the time they spent alone. It felt like it had been ages ago. She stared up at his face as he focused on the proceedings below. A smirk pulled at the corner of her lips as she turned her attention back.

"Do you, Evalyn Gemfell, have anything you wish to say on your behalf before your judgment is rendered?"

"Though it does not excuse my actions, he found me and told me he knew a way I could return to Fata Morgana with my head held high. All I had to do was help him and not ask questions. I didn't know what Alexander Fresen had planned until it was too late." The last word caught in her throat. Silence once again fell as the cloaked council members leaned in to whisper to their neighbors.

A collective hush fell as Hilda got to her feet. "You are sentenced to fifty years' imprisonment in the council cells and twenty-five years of servitude to the court. I would like to note that your punishment would have been far worse had it not been for a recommendation from King Trevan, explaining your previous exemplary service as a Steelshade."

Evalyn's aura dissolved into a deep midnight blue as her shoulders snapped into a familiar rigidity at the word. Kelly knew it too well. It was respect, pride, strength, but mostly obedience. Everything was taught to someone in the military. A weight grew in Kelly's stomach, knowing the pain and shame Evalyn felt.

CHAPTER
TWELVE

Kelly stared blankly at the paper coffee cup in her hand. Theo placed a hand on her thigh, startling her. She glanced around at the bustling crowd and leaned back on the wooden bench outside the courtroom.

"You have not said a word since we left Evalyn's sentencing. What is wrong?"

"She was a soldier?" she asked.

"Yes, a Steelshade. They are the guards that protect the fae king, much like the secret service for the president. Only Steelshades are chosen at a young age, and from what I understand, serve until their deaths."

Kelly's mind raced with even more questions now on the inner workings of supernatural politics. She glanced into Theo's dark brown eyes.

"Why is blood magic illegal? Is it just because blood is involved?"

"It is a little more complicated than that. It is considered the darkest form of magic. In order to make certain spells more effective, you have to use blood."

"Hence the name. I got that. Why is it illegal?"

"When it was first practiced, they would use the blood of an animal. Pig, goat, cow, whatever they could get. Until one Magi accidentally cut themselves. Their blood mixed with the animal blood and the spell became more powerful. Then he became obsessed with that power. Soon, they discovered that not only was human blood the most powerful but also gave the caster the ability to control the owner of the blood and influence their mind."

"Oh."

"The Magi orchestrated an elaborate plan to get the blood of high-ranking officials."

"And essentially blackmail them," Kelly finished.

"Once the Magi was captured, they had discovered their mind had become so corrupted that horrible acts like murder were as acceptable as buying a loaf of bread. All concepts of right and wrong had been erased."

The buzz of chatter in the room filled the silence that fell between them.

"Who did she use blood magic on?" Kelly asked hesitantly, a knowing knot tightened in her gut.

THIRTEEN

The crowd shifted as it began filtering into the courtroom. "It must be time." Kelly stood, tossing her still full coffee into a nearby trash can, then joined the back of the crowd as the atrium emptied.

The seats were packed. She stopped at the top of the stairs in awe at the number of people in attendance compared to the few that had been there for Evalyn, then hurried to catch up to Theo, who had already begun his descent toward the front row. Once they had reached the bottom, Kelly glanced back up at the overwhelming wall of occupants. Catching random glances and murmurs. The weight of their attention made her skin crawl. *They aren't looking at you. They aren't talking about you.* Theo touched her arm, pulling her attention as he gestured to a seat. She took it, still uncomfortably aware of every glance.

A line of people dressed in black robes poured in from a side door, followed by the council in their red robes. Kelly examined their robes, now able to see the large black sashes that drape the front, each accentuating a gold medallion around their necks.

The council again took their seats behind the curved judges' bench while the ones in black took up positions by the exits and in front of the desk. The red robe in the center stood, the crowd fell silent.

"Today we are here to witness and rule on the case involving the Magi Fiona Mackay and the crimes she is accused of," Hilda's voice boomed through the amphitheater. Valgard escorted Fiona in from the same door the council had entered. Autumn and Omari followed.

"Fiona Mackay, you stand before the council accused of illegally entering the mind of an unknowing or unwilling subject more commonly known as dreamwalking. How do you plead?"

Deafening silence filled the room and crept under Kelly's skin, wrapping around her insides. Fiona took a deep, steadying breath and lifted her gaze to the council. In that moment, Kelly saw the childlike innocence she adored melt away and, in its place, a powerful, confident woman, much like the woman who raised her.

"Guilty," she answered. The room let out a collective gasp of disbelief.

"Quiet. The council will record Ms. Mackay's plea," Hilda said, one of the other members scribbled on a piece of paper, then nodded at Hilda. "First, we will hear from Autumn Kazem, representative for the defendant, former high council member, and witness to the events," Hilda stated, returning to her seat. Autumn stepped onto the dais in the center of the floor.

"Thank you, councilor, let me first begin by putting the situation into context. My family and I were traveling to our remote summer home with a vampire yearling by the name of Eric Wilson when Fiona was targeted, then attacked by a human. Thankfully, another human intervened, saving

Fiona from using her powers in front of humans and the unsavory man. Fiona informed me that there was something different about this human, something special. Later that same evening, I got a similar report from Eli Palmer and Theodore Walsh, who ran into a woman in a nightclub. As the council is aware, Eli is able to find those that may need our guidance. The women that Fiona and Eli described were one and the same, a woman by the name of Kelly Frost. They also reported running into Vincent Bowman, a known associate of heretic Alexander Fersen." Autumn paused as the crowd broke into a flurry of concerned murmurs. Hilda held up her hand, bringing silence once again.

"Mr. Wilson expressed concern for this woman due to their relationship prior to his transition. I instructed Eli to bring her to our cabin so that we may watch over her better. After several days, it became obvious that Alexander knew something I had only suspected about her since her arrival at the cabin. He had already begun to infiltrate the woman's mind and would not stop until she was under his control," Autumn continued. Again, the crowd whispered in concern and objection.

"Ms. Kazem, please state for the council what your suspicions were," Hilda directed.

"After speaking with Ms. Frost, I had my suspicions that she had a power Mr. Fersen wanted. A rare power I had only seen a few times before."

"Were your suspicions confirmed?"

"Yes, shortly after speaking with her, Ms. Frost was then kidnapped from our campsite in the middle of the night by Mr. Wilson. It wasn't until the following morning that we discovered she was missing. To further confirm our suspicions that Alexander was behind her disappearance, we returned to her residence. Not knowing where he had taken her, time was of the essence. We couldn't wait for the council to intervene. I instructed Ms. Mackay to dreamwalk in order to find Ms. Frost."

"Why did you not do it yourself?" another member of the high council asked.

"Though I am her mentor, due to Ms. Mackay's native land, she is far more proficient."

"Thank you, Ms. Kazem. At this time, the council requests Fiona Mackay to step forward," Hilda stated. Autumn bowed her head and returned to the open seat next to Omari. Fiona walked cautiously to the dais. Keeping her eyes downcast, she stood before the high council.

"Due to this being your first appearance in front of this council, is there anything you would like to say in your defense?"

"I only wish to apologize for not waiting for authorization. I was afraid that if we didn't act quickly, Kelly, er—I mean, Ms. Frost would have died."

"In your own words, can you describe what happened during the alleged dreamwalking?"

"Yes, High Councilor." Fiona paused and closed her eyes, a pained expression written across her face. "It was dark. There was a thick fog that clung and pulled at my skin. It grew heavier as I followed the sound of her heartbeat. The closer I got to Kelly, the more the fog pulled me down, trying to keep me there. When I found her, she was lying on a wet tiled floor, covered in cuts and bruises. I touched her skin. It was colder than ice, her heartbeat growing fainter by the moment. I did my best to transfer some of my strength to her, enough to last until we could find her. The pain that she endured—" she broke off as tears streamed her cheeks.

"How long did you stay in her mind?"

"I was told I was there for less than fifteen minutes."

"Fifteen minutes? The other instances that have been brought before us were no less than an hour!" a red-cloaked member exclaimed.

Fiona's face reddened. Kelly glanced over to Theo and Omari, their expressions frozen like statues, past them Autumn beamed with pride. Kelly couldn't help but feel the tightness in her chest ease.

"Impressive, very impressive, and in that time, were you able to gather the information you needed?"

"Yes."

"Is Ms. Kelly Frost in attendance today?"

Kelly's mouth went dry. Fighting the sudden weight of her body, she got to her feet.

"I'm here, I-I am Kelly Frost."

The abundance of curious and judgmental eyes was on her, more eager and interested than before. Hilda gestured to the spot next to Fiona on the dais. Surprised that her feet could move, she stood on the spot indicated. Murmurs and questions filled the air. Fiona shot her a small, reassuring smirk.

"What would you like to see happen as a result of Ms. Mackay's actions? Knowing she invaded and manipulated your mind without your permission."

"Happen? Nothing. Though her actions were illegal by your laws, where I come from, there are laws that protect those who rescue or assist people in danger. Her actions were only done with the purest intent, and if she hadn't acted, I may have died or become bound to Alexander. I owe Fio—Ms. Mackay and her family, my life."

"So be it. Thank you, you may step down."

Kelly returned to her seat, slumping and praying something would draw attention away from her. The members of the high council got to their feet.

"The council will deliberate and return tomorrow at seven," Hilda said, then one by one the high council exited the door they had entered. The black-cloaked members stayed in their places and a steady rumble of voices grew as people discussed the case and the discoveries that unfolded. Kelly glanced down the row at Autumn, Omari, and Theo again.

"She's going to be okay, right?" Kelly asked. Theo's jaw tensed. Omari got to his feet, along with Autumn.

FOURTEEN

K elly wandered the empty athletics center holding her hair up off her neck. She had taken down her ponytail assuming it was the source of her headache before her body began oscillating between unbearably hot to uncomfortably cold. The nurse that had taken her blood had been waiting outside the courtroom with a message to report to the athletics center. At the other end of the room, the door creaked open as Jonas entered. His stern, businesslike expression and the leather portfolio reminded Kelly of a school principal. He scanned the room briefly before spotting her and raising a hand, ushering her over.

"Demand I get here immediately, then stroll in almost half an hour later and you can't even meet me halfway," she mumbled in annoyance, hastily pulling her hair back up.

"There is no time to waste. You have a lot of catching up to do."

"Catching up? Do you know what's happening to me?"

"Yes, your knowledge, or should I say lack of, is unsurprising, considering."

"What knowledge? Considering what?" she asked, ignoring the indignation.

"Does that brain of yours have other uses besides repeating what you have just heard, or are you content being a glorified parrot?"

"Perhaps if you finished a thought, or spoke to me with some respect, like an actual perso—"

"Respect is earned, not given," Jonas commanded, cutting her off.

Kelly's jaw flexed biting back her retort. Though Jonas's expression was resolute, anger flickered beneath. Jonas dragged a metal chair from the wall, passed her to the center of the room. She paused and dropped her head back before following him. *I thought I was done with chauvinistic men when I left the military.* He set his portfolio on the seat and shrugged off his tweed jacket, draping it on the chair back. Rolling up his crisp white sleeves, he stood in front of her.

"Are you going to let me know what's going on?" she said, irritated.

Jonas let out a restrained sigh. "I suppose we won't get very far otherwise. I will try to explain this as simply as possible." Kelly opened her mouth to correct his assumption, then stopped short, pressing her lips into a thin white slash. *It's not worth it right now.* "I am skeptical and still researching some other explanation. However, according to the test results, the only explanation is that you are a Conduit."

"A what?"

"A Con-du-it," he enunciated. "It is, from what I have learned and deciphered, a guardian for the human race."

"Deciphered? You're over a hundred years old, you don't know?"

"My grandfather died before he was able to teach me."

"Your grandfather?"

"Yes, it is in our bloodline. All the texts pertaining to the origin of the conduit are incomplete and written in Lepontic, the oldest Celtic language, dating back to the sixth century. It takes a great deal of time and knowledge to translate."

"Okay, why are you skeptical?"

"Because for as far back as I can find, the conduit has only ever been male."

"Do these 'ancient texts' explicitly state that?" she folded her arms across her chest.

"Not that I have found."

"So, then it is entirely possible," she concluded, an air of defiance in her tone.

"But a woman as a conduit, it's ridiculous. Women are far too delicate," Jonas scoffed. Kelly let out a heavy sigh.

"Try me," she snarled, removing her sweatshirt and tossing it to the floor.

"What is this mark?" he asked.

"I don't know. It just appeared a week or so ago."

Jonas distractedly maneuvered her wrist to get a better look at the curved edges interlocking, coming to points at the top and bottom.

Her vision went black, figures formed in the darkness surrounded by a thin fog, a child's laughter echoed hauntingly through her mind. *Come on, Margret,* the voice called. The figures became more defined: three children were running, dressed in their Sunday best. The young girl in front held a long string while the boy behind her launched a magnificent kite into the sky. A little farther back was another little girl trying to catch up. *Emily, Bran, wait for me!* Their youthful faces stretched and aged, the warm smell of a fire in a hearth filled the air. A large Christmas tree beautifully decorated appeared next to them as Emily, Margret, and Bran sat beneath it. Emily read to Margret and Bran while they each played with their toys. A bauble on the tree glowed brightly. It grew, first encompassing the tree, then the children. The room became more defined, and the scene transformed into a type of snow globe protecting the children from harm. The thick barrier between them, an apparent window into the past.

Jonas released Kelly's arm, gazing at her with a sudden and intense focus. The tension between them shifted and relaxed. He crossed to the chair and jotted down notes in his portfolio. She stared at him for a moment, seeing him in a different light. Her mind raced with questions.

"What the hell just happened?"

"I don't know," he said dismissively. The pen raced feverishly across the paper as he wrote, punctuating his internal thoughts with the occasional mumbled "fascinating" or "impossible."

"What did *you* see?" Intrigue plastered across Jonas's face, his pen at the ready.

"Uh..." Kelly closed her eyes, trying to bring back the images. "Three children, two girls and a boy flying a kite and then it was Christmas, I think, there was a tree decorated and the older girl was reading to the other two while they played with their toys. One of the ornaments on the tree turned it into a snow globe."

Jonas froze, lost in his own mind for a moment then went back to jotting notes.

"Did I miss something?" she asked.

He removed his glasses, pinching the bridge of his nose, his hand slid to his chin as he mumbled to himself.

"W-Was that your family?" she asked after another moment of silence passed between them.

Jonas stared at her as the hint of a somber memory was replaced with his normal arrogant stoicism.

Their attention turned to the door as Autumn entered.

"Ah, right," he said, clapping his portfolio closed, straightening up.

"How old were they?"

He blatantly ignored her question. "Stand here, feet shoulder-width apart. First thing is to work on your hand-to-hand combat. You cannot fulfill your duties as a conduit if you cannot defend yourself," he instructed, pointing at the spot in front of him. Kelly folded her arms across her chest.

"Now take your hand and curl your fingers into your palm, like so, be sure to place your thumb ove—" He returned the portfolio to the chair, opening it to a clean page and demonstrated how to form a fist.

"What are you doing?"

"I am showing you how to form a proper fist so that you don't break your dainty fingers when you eventually throw a punch, now—"

"I know how to punch. I know how to fight."

"What form of training did you have?" he asked, scribbling notes into the portfolio.

"I did karate as a child, but I have had one-on-one training more recently."

"And who was it that instructed you?" His eyes remained fixated on his paper.

"Why does that matter?" Kelly growled.

Autumn cleared her throat. Kelly's attention flicked to her long enough to read the message written across her face. *Behave.*

"I need to determine if it was sufficient or not," he explained, adjusting his glasses.

"Theo Walsh has been training me."

"Theodore Walsh, the vampire?" He looked up, his expression contorted to a mix of disgust and superiority. *He knows Theo?*

"Is there a problem with that? Is his training sufficient for you?" A wave of spite surged in her chest.

"Of course." A hint of condescension in his voice. "What about magic? Any experience?"

"No."

"Ms. Kazem has agreed to instruct you in defensive magic."

"And some healing," Autumn finished, approaching them.

"You know where I will be," Jonas said to Autumn, glancing once more at Kelly then marched purposefully out of the room.

"Thank God you're here, I don't know how much more of his pompous attitude or snide remarks I could take. How's Fiona? Is there any news on her sentencing?"

"She is fine, don't worry about that now. We have lots to cover. Before we begin, I have something for you." She removed a thick leather band from the folds of her dress. Taking Kelly's wrist, Autumn's brow knit as she fastened the cuff around it. A thin leather cord weaved its way around both edges, down the middle, branded runic symbols leading to the council's seal. Autumn's fingers lingering for a moment before she whispered, "Tempero." A sense of relief and rejuvenation coursed through her. Kelly opened her mouth to ask what was wrong when Autumn returned to her poised state and spoke.

"Let's begin, shall we? One of the most important things you must learn is to harness your power. Once experienced enough, you will be able to channel it in different ways, not only defensively but also offensively. We will begin by creating a shield; this will protect you in battle. However, this only pertains to magic. If you are attacked physically, your shield is useless."

"Makes sense." Kelly shrugged.

"Since this is your first time dealing with any type of magic, I will guide you through the basics, but I must warn you I will only be easy on you for the first few attempts. Place your hands like this." She pressed her palms together, leaving her index, pinky and thumb straightened. She rested her middle and ring finger over the opposite knuckles then positioned her hands so that her thumbs pressed against her chest. Kelly mirrored it but left her hands by her stomach.

"Over your heart." Autumn repositioned Kelly's hands. "The need to protect comes from the love you possess. Close your eyes," she instructed. Kelly hesitated for a moment then did.

"Do I have to do this with my hands every time?"

"No, think of it as a form of training wheels. Now picture a shield you have seen and are connected to. Got it?"

A silver police badge on a black uniform popped into her mind in the center of a navy-blue circle surrounding a blurred image. "Yes."

"Good, now imagine it between your palms, focus on every detail."

Every detail? I haven't paid attention to the details on the Maine state seal since I was a kid. It's probably fine?

"Er, okay, got it," she said, keeping her eyes closed

trying not to lose focus. The image in her mind faltered as her attention shifted to Autumn's receding footsteps.

A concentrated blow slammed into her, knocking her off balance. Her eyes shot open in time to steady herself.

"Are you picturing every detail of the shield you chose?"

"For the most part." Kelly shrugged.

"Let's try again. Remember I said every detail for a reason. The more detail, the stronger your shield will be."

She readied herself, planting her feet solidly in place. Closing her eyes again, the image of the badge returned. *Detail, detail, there is a pine tree and a dude on either side. Is that it?*

Another concentrated blow crashed into her, this time knocking her over.

"Not quite, try again."

Kelly sat up resting her elbows on her knees, Autumn standing a few feet away.

"Describe what you are picturing."

"A police badge from home."

"That won't do."

"Why not? They are guardians in a sense."

"That is true, but the conduit has been around for centuries, they are warriors. A police badge is a symbol and much too small. You need to picture something larger such as one used by Roman soldiers or medieval knights. It needs to protect you."

"How am I supposed to be connected to a shield from hundreds of years ago?"

"Throughout your life you have learned about the wars that formed your history and with it many types of armor and weapons. At some point there was one assembly that clicked in your mind, that stuck with you throughout everything."

"Okay, gimme a sec."

Snapshots of every movie scene with a shield she had ever watched with her dad fluttered through her mind like a flip book. The plain copper-colored disk wielded by the battle-ready Spartans rooted itself in her mind, punctuated with the battle scars and damage it had taken. Something hard hit her back again and she was on the floor.

"I wasn't ready," Kelly groaned, getting to her feet.

"The enemy doesn't wait for you to be ready, they attack without mercy."

"I know that, but this is training."

"I believe you are familiar with the expression 'train as you fight, fight as you train,'" Autumn said, her cocked eyebrow pulling the corner of her mouth into a smirk. Kelly let out a wry laugh.

"Alright, alright."

Her inexperience and weakness were highlighted in every bout, as her muscles twinged then ached. Kelly got to her feet, digging her nails into her palms, panting, the irritation starting to build.

"Why are you holding back?"

"I'm not holding back."

"Then why are you still being beaten by a mediocre attack? You need to defend yourself."

"I don't care what happens to me... as long as the ones I love are safe, nothing else matters."

"Ah, there you are, the benevolent protector." Autumn smiled knowingly. "This time try putting the shield in front of those you love."

She returned to her feet once more. A pair of deep brown eyes formed in her mind, staring back at her; the face started to develop around them until Theo was there in full detail. Then Autumn and Eli on either side followed by

Omari, Fiona and Kelly's parents, even her German Shepard Thor, who had positioned himself in front of Theo. Each one holding an identical shield, crouched and ready to attack.

FIFTEEN

"Come on now, wake up," Autumn coaxed. Kelly opened her eyes, staring at the dirty white and brown ceiling.

"What happened?" she rubbed her head, sitting up.

"You managed a shield for a moment before it destabilized and enhanced my attack, which then flung you back several feet." Autumn handed her a bottle of water. Taking a sip, her thirst took over. The plastic crinkle sounded as she drained its entire contents. Autumn placed a finger under Kelly's chin and examined her. "How is your head?"

"I think there's still a pebble or two rolling around, but I'll live," Kelly commented, rubbing the back of her head.

"That's enough shield training for now. Let's get you fixed up." Autumn held out her hand. Kelly took it, getting to her feet as a groan of pain reflexively slipped out.

As they left the athletics center, Kelly fell a few steps behind, every step sent a throbbing pang through her body. *There is a strong possibility something is broken.* Pressing her fingers into the back of her neck, she tried to work some of the pain away. She glanced up to see Autumn headed for the elevators instead of the clinic. Before having time to comment, Autumn had pulled the metal gate open and stepped inside. Once Kelly hobbled in, Autumn closed the gate and the elevator whirred to life. Resting her head against the wall, the subtle vibration enticed her to close her eyes and sink into a deep sleep.

A sudden jerk and loud clunk forced her body to flinch reflexively. The flash of pain caused her to suck in air through her teeth. Snapping her out of her slumberous state, *Ouch*. Autumn flashed her a wistful smirk as she stepped past Kelly and out of the elevator.

"Just a little farther, then you will feel better," Autumn said. Kelly followed her out into the lobby and headed for the door leading to the street when Autumn made an abrupt turn, crossing the lobby to a pair of narrow glass doors.

The rainlike textured glass obstructed the view of the other side. As she pushed the doors open, a rush of heavy moist air carrying the smell of rich wet soil ensnared her. The large courtyard's aged stone walls were nearly lost under the varying types of ivy and towering plants. The early afternoon sun lit the room through the immense glass ceiling. Wrought iron beams crisscrossed the glass and walls in a tangled web of elegance. Kelly stopped, drinking in the beauty of the wild and chaotic life that surrounded her. Letting the notion of stillness and tranquility breathe a rejuvenating life into the farthest reaches of her soul. Autumn drifted from one plant to another, zigzagging across the courtyard, placing bits of this and that in her basket before approaching the table in the middle.

The large wooden table was covered in glass bottles, bundles of herbs, and dried flowers. The bottles pulled her attention, their varying shapes and sizes each different from the last. Amongst the chaos, near the center of the table, sat a mortar and pestle next to a black cauldron straddling a small orange flame. Autumn began adding bits of this and a splash of that. The color-changing smoke tingled Kelly's nose as it curled its way through the air. She stepped away from Autumn and the table, taking in the surrounding area.

On each side of the table positioned a few feet away sat uniquely crafted alcoves like points on a compass. In one direction sat a white rocking chair surrounded by overflowing pots of lavender, jasmine, and baby's breath. The air around it capturing the essence of a calm summer morning. She drifted to the next alcove. This one had a chaise lounge engulfed in dazzling blue hydrangeas, next to it sat a spindly bistro table with a small waterfall on it babbling quietly. Her mind drifted to when she tried to soak her twisted her ankle in the cold river and Theo saving her from being gored. She smiled and lazily drifted to the next alcove.

Smoke poured from the mouth of an ornate stone dragon perched on top of a slender bookcase, creating a haze that clung heavily to the air around it and the elegant yet menacing wrought iron chair beside it. The shelves were filled with a rainbow of crystals of varying shapes, and sizes. As she got closer the smell of cloves filled her lungs sending a chill up her spine. There was something about this one that put her on edge. She quickly moved out of the haze and to the last alcove.

THE AIR RETURNED to the comforting smell of damp soil. A single piece of vibrant mahogany was carved into rigid, straight-backed chair. Next to it were green cage-like shelves packed with glass jars of roots, mosses, and mushrooms. One jar was filled halfway with loose dirt. Kelly stared at it. *Did it move?* Leaning closer, she watched intently, her nose only an inch away when a worm wriggled its way into sight. Kelly jumped.

"Don't tell me you are afraid of a little earth worm," Autumn smiled.

"What? Oh god no, I just wasn't expecting it."

"Come sit," Autumn said, tapping the plain wooden stool next to the table. Once Kelly sat, Autumn handed her a small unassuming bowl filled with a shimmering green liquid with strands of white inside. "Drink. All in one go is best."

"What is it?" Kelly asked, gingerly swirling it around.

"I wouldn't do that," Autumn said, watching her. "A health potion of sorts. Drink up."

She hesitated, first sniffing at it, then let out an apprehensive breath before draining the contents. The ingredients blended into an unrecognizable flavor. She held it in her mouth for a moment, trying to grab at any bit of familiarity. As she swished, the liquid grew hot. Too hot. Beginning to panic, she glanced at Autumn, who was busy gathering ingredients and selecting one of the leatherbound books. Kelly closed her eyes and gulped the almost boiling liquid. Sweltering heat coursed through her veins as the potion got to work repairing and refreshing her body. Autumn returned to the table and looked at Kelly with a flat expression.

"You swished it, didn't you?"

"What? No, I didn't," Kelly said, trying her best to look innocent. Autumn cocked an eyebrow, removing a handkerchief from her pocket.

"You're sweating. Now it's time for your next lesson."

"Next lesson? I thought we were done for today."

"I'm afraid not. Though he could have said it in a better manner, what Jonas said was true. You have lots of catching up to do in your training to become a conduit. Traditionally, your ancestors were educated one way or another throughout their lives before the council would summon them and perform the ritual, allowing them to enter our world."

"Wait, become a conduit? I thought I already was one?"

"Your bloodline gives you the foundation and the power. But control of that power is academic. Right now, your powers are growing erratically, and it will only become increasingly dangerous. You need to get control of them quickly," Autumn said, placing the large leather-bound book in front of Kelly.

"What happens if I don't?" Kelly asked, opening the book cover. Autumn's body stiffened.

"Your power will become too chaotic to control. It will begin to attack your body until your body finally gives up and you die." A heavy silence clung to the air around them. Autumn continued, "As a conduit, you have an ability no one else does and with it, a duty."

"Are you seriously giving me the 'with great power comes great responsibility' speech?"

"Your ability allows you to acquire and use aspects from supernatural creatures."

"Aspects?"

"Accelerated healing, speed, strength and such. However, with the aspects borrowed you also gain some of their weaknesses. The book before you contains different potions and instructions on how to make them."

"A cookbook," Kelly said.

"I suppose you could look at it that way. In the front are

107

some beginner ones you can read over for now. Then we will see how you do making it."

Kelly raised her hand. "What, uh, skill level is beginner exactly?"

"Standard home cook." She smiled encouragingly.

"And what if you're not a cook?"

Autumn chuckled at the thought before noticing the expression on Kelly's face. "If you're able to make, say, scrambled eggs, then you will be fine," she reassured.

Kelly's brow furrowed as she nodded. "Right, of course. And what if you burn water?"

Autumn gawked at Kelly, struggling to wrap her mind around what she had said.

"You're joking."

"I took home economics and ended up starting a fire that almost burned down my high school."

"Surely they corrected your error and continued your education."

"They dismissed our class two weeks early because of the damage. They encouraged me to find a different interest."

"Oh my. Well, I suppose we have our work cut out for us, don't we?" Autumn said, reaching for the book and flipping to the introduction page. "We will start here."

Kelly glanced at the page. At the top, large frilly letters read Potion Basics.

"All potions have three parts: base, element, and activator. Sometimes, there is an overlap of base and element. Because we are making potions and not salves or incenses, you only have four bases to work with. Those are water, syrup, vinegar, and oil."

"This says five bases: water, syrup, vinegar, oil, and

alcohol," Kelly read, following her finger across the page. Autumn's expression said it all.

"Got it, four bases."

"Including the earth's four key elements is vital for complete effect. If an element is forgotten, the potion's purpose will be fuzzy and result in unwanted side effects. Those elements are—"

"Earth, air, fire and water, right?"

"Correct."

"How do you add air? Do you just blow on it?"

"Not quite. The elements are not as straightforward as one would assume. For instance, air lacks the tangibility required for potions, so we use salt. Water can be any of the bases listed and nobody enjoys eating dirt, so we use different roots."

"But fire is fire, right? Like an actual flame?"

"In most cases, but in a pinch, you can use types of spices. Like here—" Autumn flipped a few pages forward "—in this potion you can substitute fire for cayenne pepper."

Kelly's eyes combed over the ingredients, then the steps, before she looked at the large frilly letters that read "Healing." She glanced back at the ingredients: lavender, water, mint, salt, and cayenne pepper. Then scanned the steps until she spotted a note at the bottom of the page.

Once the potion has reached its finished state and color, DO NOT AGITATE.

"Is this what you gave me?"

"With a few adjustments, but yes. Now it's your turn to make it. There is no flame required to make this, so you should be fine," Autumn said, taking a step back from the table, gesturing.

Kelly hesitated, then picked up the book and traded places with Autumn. The sour taste of bile crept up her throat and, with it, the memories of all her failed attempts at cooking. She could feel the sweat pooling between her hands and the covers of the book. Setting it on a small empty space, she wiped her hands on her pants and glanced up at Autumn, who watched her patiently with a content smile.

Kelly read the page one more time before she began, then read every step and every measurement three times before moving on to the next. Every few minutes she would glance over at Autumn, still perched on the stool composed as if no time had passed. Once finished, Autumn leaned forward.

"Fantastic! See, I knew you could do it. Shall we try something a little harder?"

"Uh." Kelly stared. "But I only did it once."

"Yes, you'll have plenty of time to practice later. For now, empty the cauldron into this flask. Then we will move on," Autumn said, handing her an old flask similar to the one Theo carried. Kelly poured the potion into the flask as Autumn flipped toward the back of the book, stopping on a tattered page covered in varying unknown stains and splotches of ink. Its original title *Essence* crossed out and below it scratched in a familiar handwriting *Transmutation*. A long, ragged cut in the middle of the page was poorly taped back together. Several of the ingredients had been scribbled out and replaced with another, only to have it replaced once more. The measurements and steps followed the same confused pattern.

"It is critical you get this one accurate."

"What will happen if I don't?" she asked, forcing a small lump down her throat.

"It will be extraordinarily painful. Don't worry about it now. Let's get to work. Most of the ingredients are on the black shelves."

Kelly grabbed the few the ingredients she could decipher and went back to the table. Autumn had returned to the cauldron, relighting the fire beneath.

"I got the ones I could make out."

"Excellent. You can get started while I get the remaining few items. Remember, it must be exact, any more or less could cause an unwanted result," she said over her shoulder as she headed off deeper into the conservatory. Kelly watched as Autumn disappeared into the overgrown greenery.

"Fuck," she breathed, placing the jars on the table and focused on the first step.

Add water and ash mixture to hot iron potjie.

"Okay, going to assume that is a potjie. Next, add water and ash mixture, easy enough." Kelly scanned the table, spotting a tall triangular bottle labeled "water" then glanced at the recipe. *One- and one-half gills.* "Gills? What the fuck is a gill? A gallon? Probably not, think metric. A gram? That can't be right, a gram of water." Kelly glanced around, searching for any sign of Autumn. She let out a frustrated grumble. "Fuck it, it's only water. I'm sure it will be fine." Then added just enough water to cover the bottom. "Now for the ash mixture, how much? Wait, what is it mixed with?" she muttered as her finger zoomed across the page.

*In a mortar stir, One thought of ash with One dash of acacia,
rotating to the west three times.*

"You have got to be fucking kidding me," she growled, her frustration growing. The mortar made a heavy bang as she placed it in front of her, then scoured the jars on the table. With the jar of ash in one hand and a jar of acacia in the other, Kelly poured some of each into the mortar. Picking up the mortar in both hands, spun counterclockwise three times, then added the mixture into the water. She watched as the boiling water dissolved the ash.

Gingerly add two drams of beet juice.

"Okay, beets. Beets. Beets. Where are the beets?" she mumbled, searching the cluttered table. Just then, Autumn returned, placing a dark red beet and a small brown bottle on the table.

"You seem to be getting along well," Autumn said, smiling as she glanced into the cauldron.

"How much is two drams?"

"Oh, only a splash," Autumn said, slicing the beet into chunks and placing them in the mortar and handing the pestle to Kelly. She stared blankly at Autumn, then at the pestle.

"Do you have a splash spoon or cup?" Kelly asked, trying to contain her sarcasm.

"You can use this; two drams is roughly half. Make sure you crush those up well. Chunky potions are never good," Autumn said, handing Kelly something similar to the plastic cup that comes with cold medicine. Kelly mashed and add the beet juice.

Add one knob or one pony of essence, then let simmer for one turn of the hourglass.

"I am assuming a pony is not an actual small horse?"

"You are correct. A pony is a liquid measurement," Autumn said as she poured the contents of the brown bottle into the cauldron and turned the small hourglass hidden amongst the clutter.

"So what, uh, creature am I going to become?"

"You will see," Autumn teased, ladling some into the same bowl she had used for the health potion. Kelly followed Autumn away from the table. She then handed the bowl to Kelly. "All in one go."

Kelly let out a reluctant sigh and chugged it. The potion dragged its way down her throat, first causing her ears to grow increasingly hot, then her chest became ice cold. Her muscles turned to jelly, sending her crashing to the floor. She tried to fight back as her body convulsed. *Oh god, is this how I die?* As the convulsions subsided, an odd sensation crept across her body like thousands of snakes wriggling around under her skin. She gulped at the air, failing to fill her lungs. Autumn leaned over her as she lay helpless on the floor.

"Your proportions are off," Autumn said, pouring the flask of health potion into Kelly's mouth.

"You think!" Kelly snapped once able to catch her breath. "What kind of measurement is a thought, anyway?"

"Let's try again," Autumn said, helping Kelly to her feet and returning to the table.

CHAPTER

SIXTEEN

K elly let out a groan as she pulled her shirt over her head. "Some health potion," she scoffed. Twisting one way, then the other, the muscles in her back screamed in protest. *I haven't been this sore in years.* Resting her head in her hands, she closed her eyes. *They need to list side effects on those recipes.* A sudden *tap tap tap* on the door caused her to jerk, sucking in a sharp breath through her teeth. *Son of a...* Gritting her teeth, she crossed her room and flung open the door.

"The council has reached a verdict; they are gathering now," Theo said. His eyes caught her attention; normally chocolate brown, they were now large black saucers. His familiar warm energy was dulled but still there beneath the surface, like the weight of the world was on his shoulders. *He probably hasn't eaten much since the trial started.* Kelly winced as she grabbed the sweatshirt off her bed, throwing it over her head as he closed the door behind them. "Are you alright?"

"Yeah, fine, just feel like I went ten rounds with Floyd Mayweather. Where have you been?"

"With Fabian."

"Is that good or bad?"

"It is complicated. There is a lot to go over between what happened with Eric and Alexander."

Kelly stopped, grabbing his forearm and pulling him to face her.

"Is he saying it's your fault? Because it's not, I'll go to bat for you."

"Go to bat?" His brows furrowed.

"It means I'm on your side. I'll tell him what happened myself."

"I thank you for the offer, darling, but I'm afraid it would all be in vain." He gave her a feeble smile.

"What do you mean?"

"Fabian does not hold humans in high regard."

"If there is anything I can do..."

"I will tell you. About the date I promised you—"

"Kelly, Theo!" Autumn called, briskly waving them over from across the atrium as the crowd swallowed her. Theo let out a restrained sigh.

"What's wrong?"

"Nothing. We can talk after the verdict," Theo replied, his voice tinged with sadness.

"Are you sure? I don't care if we are late."

"No, it is fine. There is still time," he sighed.

Kelly tilted her head, making strong eye contact. He gave her a halfhearted smile, then pecked her on the lips. A small tightness formed in her chest. She snaked her fingers into his, gripping his hand firmly, trying to express that everything would be okay while hiding her own trepidation.

By the time they reached their seats, most of the crowd was settled in theirs. The black-cloaked council members and Fiona had returned to their positions. Autumn and Omari headed for the dais when a black-cloaked member stepped away from their post to intercept them. Autumn held her head high, shooting the person beneath a challenging gaze, stopping them in their tracks. Autumn and Omari joined Fiona on the dais. The string of red-cloaked high council members filed in.

"They are back early. That's good, right?" Kelly whispered.

"Not necessarily," Theo replied in an ominous tone.

"What's the worst thing they could do to her?"

The high council stood in front of their seats, all of their cowls obscuring their faces except for Hilda. An unsettling hush washed over the crowd.

"Fiona Mackay, you have broken one of the cardinal laws set in place by the Council of the Eternals. Though your actions were noble, we cannot allow it to go without repercussions. Therefore, you are sentenced to five years' imprisonment with the possibility of council service after your first year pending good behavior. This case is closed," Hilda declared. The high council filed out of the room, followed by the remaining black-cloaked members. The crowd got to their feet, heading for the exits. Two black cloaks approached Fiona, Autumn, and Omari as they left the dais.

"I will speak with the high council, don't worry. I love you," Autumn said, kissing Fiona on the forehead. Fiona's fingers slipped from Omari's as the guards ushered her out the door. Kelly's stomach dropped. *This is all my fault.*

"Don't worry, she will be alright," Theo stumbled over the word don't.

"Ms. Frost." The petite nurse approached from the other

side of the room. "You are to report to the athletics center immediately."

"But... I..."

The woman pulled on Kelly's arm, dragging her away from Theo and his crestfallen expression. The crowd filled the growing space between them as they headed for the exits, discussing the verdict and other events of the day. Crossing the threshold before the door swung shut, she saw a red-cloaked member of the high council approach Theo.

CHAPTER
SEVENTEEN

After drifting around the athletics center for longer than she liked, Kelly grabbed the back of the metal chair still untouched from her session with Jonas, spun it to face the door, then plopped down, stretching out her legs. *This is beginning to get ridiculous.* Her eyes landed on a worn-out part of her shoe as her mind slipped back across the sea, back to her front porch in Maine, with Theo next to her and Thor by her feet, listening to the quiet hum of the day. The memory of rain shifted her thoughts to the cabins. Theo's face lit by the moon as the clouds cleared. An otherworldly beauty. She let herself imagine what their future could be like before a deflating weight took root in her gut. *If only.*

Her thoughts were cut short by Autumn entering, followed by two men dressed similar to the guard from the cells, leading a chained, clean and plainly dressed Evalyn. One guard removed the shackles from her wrists. Underneath them were large leather bracers adorned with an intricate metal design.

"What is she doing here?" Kelly hissed as she shot up from her seat.

"As part of Evalyn's sentencing, the council has decided she is to help train you in the ways of psychic tenacity."

"Psychic what?"

"I'm going to teach you how to mentally protect yourself from adversaries," Evalyn clarified.

"Why can't you or Omari teach me?" Kelly directed the question at Autumn.

"There is no one better," Evalyn interjected.

"It will help you get the control you need to endure your innate magic. I have matters I must attend to. I will be by later," Autumn said, exchanging a glance with Evalyn. She gave a quick nod in response, adjusted her bracers and headed for the center of the room. "Don't worry, those bracers are specially crafted to subdue her powers. You are perfectly safe."

"Autumn."

"Yes, dear?"

"I wanted to apologize to you, Omari, and especially Fiona."

"Whatever for?" Autumn asked, puzzled.

"It's my fault your family isn't together. It's my fault Fiona got into trouble."

"No, my dear, it's what we do. We protect the ones we care about."

"But—"

Autumn gave her a comforting smile. Kelly stood speechless, watching Autumn disappear from the room. Evalyn sat straight-backed and cross-legged, with her hands resting in her lap in the middle of the floor.

"Why do you assume there is 'no one better'? Is it because you are a Steelshade?" Kelly asked, making her way over to her. The smoke-like aura around Evalyn turned a violent red, rolling and lapping at the air like a stormy sea. Her body went rigid like it had during her sentencing.

"No." The room filled with a heavy silence. "I have been there before," Evelyn said.

"In someone's mind? So, what?"

"In *your* mind," Evelyn clarified. Kelly's mind raced.

"Alexander's basement. It was you. You twisted my memories and turned them against me." Kelly's anger grew as she pulled the pieces together. "I was half dead; it couldn't have been that difficult to take advantage of."

"Didn't you ever wonder about your dreams? How they felt wrong? Like they weren't yours?"

Kelly's body went rigid. *I never told anyone about that, not even Theo.*

"Alexander forced me to use blood magic to control you through your dreams. He knew from the beginning that was going to be the only way you would consider joining him."

"The restaurant," Kelly concluded. "The look you gave me while you treated my hand. You even said, 'with the right man you could rule the world' and you are really trying to convince me he forced you? That's bullshit and you know it!"

"What you think you saw, and the truth, are not the same," Evelyn barked, springing to her feet.

"Then why don't you enlighten me?"

A frown creased Evelyn's forehead.

"It was around thirteen months ago in Los Angeles. We were there searching for a weapon. At least, that's what Alexander told us."

"What kind of weapon?"

"I don't know. No one did. All he told us was we would know when we found it. He hid it so well." The crease on her forehead grew deeper. "One night he'd send a group out for supplies, the next night recruits, then the weapon. Just when we figured out the pattern, he'd change it. The groups too."

"How did you land on me? I was nothing special, a normal human."

"You are far from normal. Haven't you noticed the odd, even frightened looks you get from us?"

"I didn't give it much thought," Kelly lied.

"It's your aura."

"What about it?"

"You don't have one. Well, you didn't. Now it's—" She shuddered.

"What?"

"Black, but not just black, but the unsettling weight of death, an endless void of darkness. When you were still unaware of us, you didn't have one."

"What do you mean I didn't have one? That's impossible, isn't it?"

"Now you're catching on. Your aura was clear like water, but it didn't just surround you, it surrounded the people close to you. It would mix with theirs, making it impossible to locate the source."

Kelly looked confused.

"There was a time you were with Eric and a few others. The aura around all of you became the same, a swirling, fluctuating crimson red and midnight blue." Evelyn paused. "They assumed it was coming from Eric. Once Alexander discovered the mistake, he punished us all and tortured Eric for your information." Evelyn stared off into the distance, lost in her memories.

"I still don't understand why it has to be you," Kelly muttered sorely.

"I'm a Fae, my magic is rooted in the elements and because of that, I am naturally more powerful than your friends."

"Fae, is that like a fairy?"

"What you know as fairies is so misconstrued; it is astounding you evolved as much as you have. Fairy is a name, the insultingly weak name humans labeled us when they found a group of our children playing. Our children, much like human children, only see the goodness in the world. The humans then took advantage of their kindness." Evalyn's aura dissolved into a deep red.

"Okay, Tinkerbell, relax. It was just a question."

"I don't have to help you, you anorexic gorilla," Evalyn snapped. Kelly glanced over her shoulder at the guard near the door as he shifted his weight.

"Then why are you?"

"He took something of mine. I want them back."

"What was it?" Kelly asked. Evelyn's aura shifted once again, this time to the same deep blue as her sentencing. A sinking weight filled Kelly's chest. *You catch more flies with honey,* her mother's voice echoed in her mind. "Soldier to soldier," Kelly finished fragilely. Evelyn's rigidness softened as if acknowledging that out of everyone, maybe, just maybe, she might understand.

"My tonfas. Steelshades begin their training as children. Once they are old enough, they have to complete the Cestus. It's a series of trials that gauge your ability to protect the realm. Once completed, you are given your assignment. The ones that perform the best are assigned to the king and given a pair of tonfas made from our sacred Hawthorne tree. Losing them is the human equivalent of treason and genocide combined. Without them, I can never return home."

"How long has it been?" Kelly asked. Evelyn stared off into the distance. *Too long.*

"So, er, where do we start?" Kelly asked.

"I was informed you are a conduit. Is that correct?"

"I guess so."

"Interesting. Autumn has also told me you have done some shield training. So, this should be easier for you than most. Take a seat," Evelyn gestured to the area on the floor. "Close your eyes and picture your spark."

"My spark?"

"Yes, your spark, your life essence, the thing that makes you who you are."

"You mean my soul?"

"I suppose that could be the same for a human."

"Okay." Kelly took a deep breath, released it slowly, and closed her eyes. *My spark. My soul... Does a soul have a shape? What kind of shape? Animal, mineral, plant? What if the shape is bad? Like a slug or a blobfish.* Kelly's eyes shot open. *I don't want to be a blobfish.*

"What exactly does a soul look like?" Kelly asked.

"It's different for everyone."

"Humor me, I got thrown into the deep end without knowing how to swim."

"Try to imagine the flame of a candle in the palm of your hand."

Kelly closed her eyes. *Okay, my spark, the flame of a candle, my spark, the flame of a candle.* Searching the darkness of her mind, her chest grew tight. *Why can't I picture it? I know what a flame looks like.* Kelly let out a frustrated grunt. *Let's start with a spark. What makes a spark? A lighter.* The familiar *flick* echoed in her head. *What makes me, me?* The photo from her bedside table back home came into focus. She and Eric, thousands of miles from home, surrounded by an endless sandscape and impending hostility. Yet, still finding the ability to laugh. *Flick, flick.* She pictured sparks coming from the flint wheel of a plastic BIC but quickly fizzling out.

"Focus," Evalyn said. Kelly furrowed her brow. The image slowly moved, swirling into her memory.

"Anyone got a light?" a phantom voice called.

"Yeah. Here," her own voice echoed. Sparks flew from the lighter, then disappeared again in an instant. She tried once more, cupping the lighter from the nonexistent wind this time. The flame formed, caressing the butt of the cigarette. As it pulled away, the flame danced before settling. The warmth expanded across her palm as the memory around it faded into blackness, and only the flame remained.

Holding it near her face, she fixated on it. The small flame hovered an inch above her palm, bobbing only slightly. The longer she stared, the more the light pulled at her heart, drawing itself into her chest. A familiar heat crawled up her arms, caressing her skin.

"Now make a shield around it, protect it," Evelyn's distant voice instructed. The image of the battered Spartans' shield appeared in front of the flame.

"Okay, got it." As the words left Kelly's lips, the flame was blown out.

"Not quite. Your shield needs to protect from all sides. Try again."

They continued on for what felt like hours. Kelly would picture the flame and Evelyn would snuff it out. With every round, the flame appeared faster until it was ingrained.

Several times, she had blocked Evelyn's attacks, only for her to change tactics.

~

"ONE MORE TIME," Kelly begged in determination.

"That's enough for today. You are beginning to get sloppy."

"I just need a break, five minutes."

"Fine, five minutes, but this will be the last time for the day."

"Oh, I am sorry, do you have somewhere else to be?" Kelly jabbed. Evelyn glared at her. "It was just a joke," Kelly said, stretching out on the floor, staring at the ceiling. A few moments of silence passed before a thought occurred.

"How did someone in such a place of honor end up in league with a piece of scum like Alexander?"

"I ran into him several times during my time in the royal guard. I was an attaché for His Royal Highness King Trevan of Fata Morgana. Every time, he would claim the council was keeping him unlawfully locked away because they feared him. At first, his stories were like childish babble, declaring the council wasn't preparing for the future and the leadership had become corrupt—imprisoning those trying to overthrow the high council. I didn't believe him until the human world began putting cameras in phones and on street corners. Our world was rapidly shrinking, and I had a duty to protect my king and my home." Evelyn fell quiet as her misguided actions replayed in her mind.

"Let's do this one more time," Kelly said, breaking the silence. She returned to her position, rolling her shoulders a few times, and closed her eyes.

It's my spark, not some museum piece. It's me. She tried to picture the flame encompassing her skin like armor. But the flame danced, only splitting from one to two. *Come on, you've got this.* She pictured the first night at the cabins, the way the flames had licked Autumn's skin when she crossed the campfire. Slowly twisting the image until the flames danced across her own skin. *Something's not right. What's missing?* As her irritation welled, her mind drifted to the small clearing in the forest, scattered beams of light cascading across the forest floor, Theo standing in front of her, adjusting her form. An intense heat emanated around her fist and followed his fingertips as they caressed their way up her arm and across her shoulders. The heat trickled down her spine and wrapped her torso. She took a steadying breath.

Kelly opened her eyes, the intense heat still radiating through her. Something flickered in the corner of her eye. Glancing down, a thin layer of blue flame surrounded her.

"Holy shit," she breathed, springing to her feet, feverishly patting the flames.

"How... interesting," Evelyn breathed in awe.

EIGHTEEN

Kelly's pace slowed in the midday sun; it seemed like the first time in days that she wasn't escorted or rushed from one place to another. The heat of the sun danced across her exposed skin. She had showered and changed after the training with Evalyn and chose to leave her jacket back in her room. *I wonder where Theo is. I need to talk to him. This is all so much to process.* She lazily climbed the steps to Jonas's. Opening the door, loud, tense voices carried from behind Jonas's closed study door. *Who's in there? That voice.* She crept down the hall, leaning her ear close enough to make out what the two were arguing about.

"Is Kelly here?" Theo asked.

"Not at the moment," Jonas responded in an aloof tone.

"Where is she?" Theo asked, not hiding his frustration.

"I cannot see how that's any of your concern."

"I need to speak with her."

"I'm sure whatever you need to say can wait or be put into a letter."

"No, it cannot. It is too important. It would be better in

person," Theo said. His footfalls grew fainter, then louder. *Why is he pacing?*

"It would be better for you to bow out of her life," Jonas snapped, punctuating his sentence and mood with the thump of his book closing.

"It is her choice who is in her life."

"She is my charge, a child, and knows nothing of our world. I will not let her be fooled by your deception," Jonas snapped.

"I have never deceived anyone. Especially after breaking Alexander's hold over me."

"Omission of events is still deception."

A heavy pause filled the air, years of pain bubbling between them. Theo let out a deep sigh.

"We are of the same world. Do you really still harbor such contempt toward me?" The dejected tone of Theo's voice gnawed at Kelly's insides. She pressed her ear firmly against the door.

"I always will. After her death, you disappeared without a word." Jonas's words dripped with resentment.

"It has been over one hundred forty-three years, Jonas."

"When you finally did emerge again, you were a blood-thirsty monster. The devastation you left in your wake is unforgivable."

"I spent fifty years in the council cells trying to atone for sins done by my hand. Those actions will always haunt me, never allowing me to be free. I see each of their faces every day. It is not your place to judge whether I have suffered enough."

"They were children!" Jonas's voice broke.

"And I will never forgive myself," Theo said, throwing the door open. Kelly's weight shifted, stumbling forward into Theo. Jonas sprang to his feet.

"Kelly!" he exclaimed. Regaining her balance, she pushed Theo away, looking up into his shocked expression. "I was looking for you. We—"

"You lied to me," she accused, her tone a mix of anger and incredulity, trying to wrap her mind around everything.

"You see, I told you, leav—" Jonas interjected. Kelly's head snapped in Jonas's direction as she advanced on him.

"You don't get even a whisper of a say in my life, treating me like some servant whose only job is to cater to your every need. Someone who couldn't possibly know as much as you. You don't know me. I served in the military. Fought for my country. I saw combat. I'm every bit as equal to you, to any man!" she shouted, all of her bottled-up anger boiling over. Theo's hand grabbed her elbow. Kelly wheeled around, ripping it away.

"And you! For weeks I have been obsessing over that journal, hoping to find an answer to what is happening to me ever since the ritual and Alexander's. You knew the one person who could help me was alive and well. The whole fucking time!" She was shouting again, her voice growing horse and scratchy with every word. Glaring up into his eyes, those comforting eyes that were her escape now enraged her, turning to an ache in her chest. She shoved past him, storming the hall. Throwing the door open.

"Kelly, hey, I was jus—" a baffled Eli stood before her.

"Did you know?" she barked.

"Know what?" he asked, a little bewildered. His gaze went from her to Theo standing in the open doorway. She blew past him in a cloud of rage. Eli gave a small nod to Theo, then chased after her, jogging a bit to catch up, then effortlessly kept pace. They reached the entrance to the council. Kelly didn't slow. She crossed the street, dodging traffic.

"Kelly, wait. What the hell is going on?" Eli demanded, grabbing her arm and spinning her to face him.

"He lied, he knew, and he fucking lied!"

"Who knew what?" Eli asked, trying to grasp what was happening. She glanced behind him. They were standing at the entrance to the Palace of Versailles. A sense of unease and familiarity pulled at her. Transfixed on the palace, she passed through the large entrance gate, weaving her way through the scattered crowd in the courtyard and headed toward the entrance.

"Kelly, what is going on?" Eli pleaded. She ignored him. The rooms passed in a blur of color, history and observers. At the bottom of the queen's staircase, Eli caught up enough to grab Kelly's forearm and spin her around. "Stop, okay, just stop. What the hell is going on?" Eli said, confused.

"I-I don't know. I have never been here in my life, but it's so familiar." Her brow wrinkled as she glanced up the stairs and continued up them at almost a run.

"Kelly, wait!" Eli shouted. Random voices gasped and commented as she forced her way past them.

Kelly stopped in the center of a seemingly endless hall. A surge of terror ran through her, rooting her feet in place, turning her blood cold. *Floor-to-ceiling mirrors, golden statues.* A haunting laugh echoed in her mind. The nightmare came back in flashes. A golden throne. Fancy ruffled dresses. Red scarfs turning to blood. A hand touched her shoulder. She whirled around, ready to fight or run, only to be met with the concerned face of Eli. He scanned her panicked expression and, without a word, wrapped his arms around her.

"You are safe," he whispered as she buried her face in his shoulder. They stood there for a few moments until he felt Kelly's rigidity dissolve. "Let's get out of here," he coaxed, leading her back down the stairs and out of the palace in silence. Once they exited the gates, Kelly paused for a moment, glancing once more at the palace, then toward Jonas's house and the council.

"Theo knew about Jonas; he's known him forever, and he lied to me about it," Kelly said. Her eyes locked on the street as if waiting for one of them to appear.

"Wait. What?" Eli said. Kelly turned her back to the council and started searching around.

"What are you looking for?"

"A bus, subway, taxi. I don't care. I just need to get away from here right now."

"This way." Eli gestured toward the subway station. "Jonas is... he's the head of the council's law enforcement. I think he's a witch or something. He's also my new boss. I am not surprised Theo knows him."

"And?"

"And what? That's all I know."

"You don't know, do you?" she realized.

"That's what I said," he said, flashing a playful grin. They spotted the sign for the subway station and descended to the platform. Eli paid for their tickets. They went through the barrier and waited on the platform with the slowly building crowd. Subway train brakes let off an ear-splitting screech as the train came to a stop. Stepping onto the train, Eli gestured to an open seat. Kelly shook her head, then held on to the nearest pole. Eli plopped into the seat nearest her.

"What about the journal?" she asked him, breaking the silence.

"You have a journal? Oh, what a girl," he winked. "Theo said you had one. I just assumed it was your own."

"No, it was my ancestor's."

"Oh, well, that's still—"

"Jonas Wainwright," she said, raising her eyebrows.

"Oh, okay. I see. It makes sense now."

"He's not a witch either. He's a conduit and apparently I'm one, too."

"What's a Conduit?"

"Fucked if I know, some kind of soldier or something. Where are we going?"

"I am kidnapping you," Eli joked.

"Haha, very funny. Really, where are we going?"

Eli stood, took out his phone, and flicked on his flashlight. He shined it in each of her eyes, flicking it away, then back. He pinched one of her cheeks. When she yelped in pain, he pretended to look down her throat.

"My prognosis: too much Voodoo, not enough Woohoo," he said, throwing his hand into the air and jiggling around to nonexistent music. "If it isn't treated immediately, I'm afraid the consequences will be dire," he said, making a stereotypical Sigmund Freud impression.

"What does that translate to?"

"You got a whole lot of traumatic and weird shit put on your plate all at once and no time to breathe, so you and I are going to spend the day doing lame, touristy, *human* things."

"That sounds great," she smiled.

"Before we begin, there are some rules to this human-only day. First, no talk of supernatural or immortal beings. We can't have fun if we are worrying about that stuff."

Kelly looked around the subway car. Several people were looking at them with odd expressions on their faces.

"Okay, what else?"

Eli paused and scratched his head, then shrugged. "That's it, really."

"Just one rule, then?"

"Yup, but considering everything, it's a doozy."

"Fine. But before that you need to tell me how you are doing? I didn't see you after Alexander's, and that was a bloodbath." An old woman got up from her seat, taking the hand of the young girl with her and ushered her into the next car. Eli and Kelly exchanged glances and erupted in laughter.

"That's the only exception, but we can talk about that when there are less people around," he said.

They made small talk as the subway hurtled through the dark tunnels. After about an hour, Eli got out of his seat and darted on to the platform and up the stairs. She took off after him.

"Where are we?" she asked, catching up to him at the top of the stairs.

"Paris," he announced, holding up his arms in a big reveal. She scanned the buildings, looking for an indication that would confirm it was Paris, when her eyes landed on a building in the distance.

"Is that—" she broke off.

"Notre Dame," he finished. She stared as they made their way to the courtyard filled with tourist groups in matching shirts, school children on a class trip, locals having a quick lunch and even a man on bended knee proposing to his girlfriend. Kelly noticed an empty spot on a nearby stone bench. They sat in silence for a while, drinking in the historic beauty displayed before them. Kelly's mind raced; the humbling nature of the church's architecture brought back feelings and memories she had thought were gone.

"Do you believe there is an afterlife?" she said, her voice catching in her throat at the memory of Eric, her former best friend, playing in the forefront of her mind.

"I don't know, I like not knowing. Eric is at peace, not in pain or under someone's control. That's all that matters."

"I guess you're right," she smiled weakly, wiping away the single tear from her cheek.

"Come on, we have a lot to see."

Kelly stared up at the humbling architecture one last time, then she and Eli headed off down the street. They passed by a handful of small cafés and bookstores before one caught her eye. A large window filled with wind chimes, crystal dream catchers and other new age items illuminated by a neon pink sign that spelled out psychic. She raked over the trinkets in the window, musing over how, not that long ago, she thought it all to be a load of crap and people claiming to be psychics were just good at reading body language. But now, here she was, thrust into the center of a world society had told her didn't exist. As her gaze moved from one end of the display to the other, she landed on the two printed signs next to the door, one in French, the other in English. Large red letters read, "MISS-ING." The photo beneath was of a kind-faced man in his late twenties, his black hair neatly cut, his green eyes barely visible behind his charming smile. It must have been a happy day. Below the picture was the man's information: *Caleb Sagelight, green eyes, black hair, six foot two, last seen...* Kelly froze.

"What, you want your fortune told? That's a little hokey even for me."

"No, it's not that," Kelly said, pointing to the missing person sign.

"Do you know him?"

"No, the date last seen. That's..." She clenched her eyes closed, thinking hard, trying to pull back the memory of the sign from Delirium. "That's a week after Chris Bradtree."

"Did you know that person?"

"No, but doesn't it seem strange?"

"How? People go missing all the time. Come on, I want to show you something," Eli said, taking a couple of steps down the road. Kelly didn't follow, instead she entered the shop.

The shop was dimly lit. The ceiling and walls were covered in multicolored scarfs and tapestries, all displaying varying religious symbols. She recognized a couple like the Hindu symbol for Om, the tree of life and the Wiccan pentacle. But then there were others she could only guess at. The sweet, woody, musky smoke clung to the air, filling Kelly's senses, making her calm and even a little sleepy. She passed by a rack of scarfs and cloth bags. Next to it sat a table covered in meditation CDs, silver earrings and jewelry, worry stones, crystals and other odd knickknacks. At the end of the table sat a display of different tarot cards, from classic to mythical creatures. A few were fanned out to show the beautiful artwork on one deck. One card caught her eye.

"The magician, it can stand for power, potential, and even the unification of the spiritual and physical worlds," a woman said behind her.

"I'm sorry?" Kelly replied, turning around to face where the voice came from. The woman barely reached Kelly's chin. Her black curls only tamed by the deep purple kerchief tied around her head. The plain white top cinched by a large corset-style belt around her waist separated the many vibrant scarves that had been draped over the skirt, making Kelly think of a painter's color wheel. The woman's gaze raked over Kelly's casual, more modern appearance. She locked eyes with Kelly, a sense of fealty flowed from her. Without breaking away, she tapped her long index finger on the card Kelly had been staring at. The woman's emerald eyes felt heavy with a lifetime of knowledge.

"You are the nexus, though you may not see it just yet. You have suffered. I am sorry to inform you, but it will not be the last. The world will become soaked in blood and turn the darkest black before you are able to see the light. Do not shy away from the blood, it will keep you safe. It is your only shield." The woman gripped Kelly's elbow, adding an unsettling level of desperation to her cryptic message. The bell above the door tinkled as it opened.

"Kelly, are you okay?" Eli asked, seeing the woman holding on to her.

"Yeah, everything is fine," Kelly said distractedly. The woman released her elbow and folded her hands in front of her.

"I am Mabel Sagelight. Welcome to my shop. How may I help you?"

"Er, yeah, I actually just wanted to ask you about the sign in your window... the missing person?" Kelly stumbled, trying to remember why she had come in.

"That is my grandson, Caleb."

"Is he... are you..."

"Yes, unlike the droves of people claiming to be psychics, we actually are."

"No offense, but can you prove it?" Kelly asked. The woman picked up a bundle of tightly wrapped herbs and lit it, wafting the smoke around Kelly. Once she circled her, she stepped back, looking at her like a stylist working on a new outfit. Her eyes darted to Eli, then back.

"Your aura is unique; it is like a void or absence of one. You could adapt anyone's to be your own for a while. His is vivid, strong, faithful, loyal," she said, shooting a wink at Eli, "he's a lover, not a fighter. Keep him close."

"Where did your grandson go missing from?"

"Out front, he was locking up for the night."

"Have the police had any leads?"

"No, and I don't expect they will."

"Why do you say that?"

"There is something dark coming, something ancient. This is only the beginning." She shuddered, stuffing a vial into Kelly's hand. Eli pulled Kelly's arm.

"Come on, let's go," he whispered. Kelly glanced once more at the woman, then left the shop with Eli.

They bounded off down the street. Eli led the way while Kelly's mind churned. The interaction with Mabel, the missing person signs, the intruders during the night, only getting the briefest reprieve when Eli would crack a joke or bring up something mundane. They hailed a cab; Eli told the driver where to go in French. Kelly stared out the window as Paris' historic and modern beauty was painted with the magnificent colors of the setting sun, making her surroundings something truly unique.

The cab stopped as they clambered out. Kelly looked up at the momentous Eiffel Tower. Eli led her over to a door next to the entrance and flashed some kind of pass at the security guard. The security guard escorted them onto the rather crowded elevator car, then said something to Eli in French. Kelly eyed him as the doors closed and he turned his head, speaking into his walkie talkie. The gears shuddered and clacked, while giant steel beams passed the large windows as the car glided along the track. Once the car stopped, they followed the crowd onto the platform. Eli snaked his arm through Kelly's and wheeled her into a second empty car. She looked at Eli, confused.

The elevator chimed, and as the doors opened, Kelly and Eli stepped out. The observation deck was empty except for the one worker under a sign that read "Champagne." Eli got two flutes from the man and handed one to her. Leaning on the railing, they watched as the last glimpse of daylight darkened with a finale of color and the lights below flicked on like fireflies on the warm summer night.

"What do I do?"

"Take it one step at a time. That's all you can do."

"It's just so overwhelming. What happened back home was like taking a sip from your parent's wine glass. This... this is like chugging a fifth of vodka while balancing on one foot."

"Yeah, I suppose it is." Eli laughed. He wrapped an arm around her shoulder.

"You never answered my question."

"What's that?"

"How are you? After everything that went down at Alexander's."

"I'm alright. I went home and saw my family. It was nice, but I felt so out of place. Like I didn't belong there anymore. The people that I had to kill, I still see their faces. I know you said not to, but I think of them as people. I can't see what you do. They have no fangs, no pointed ears, pale skin, nothing. To me, they are as normal as you and I."

"I'm sorry. I cannot begin to imagine what that must be like."

"I'm working through it. I just need to keep my friends

close," he said, shaking her shoulder. The ache in her chest that she had ignored since storming out of Jonas's surged.

"What do I do, Eli? How can I learn from Jonas when he treats me like less than a person and how can I trust Theo, knowing he lied to my face for weeks?"

"I am sure there is a reason Theo didn't tell you about Jonas. You should ask him."

Kelly opened her mouth to interject.

"And listen to what he has to say," he finished. She smiled, nudging him in the ribs. "As for Jonas, he will see in time how intelligent and strong you are."

"We should head back," she said, stifling a yawn.

"Are you going to get some sleep or talk to Theo?" he asked as they headed back to the elevator.

"Sleep. I will talk to him in the morning."

"Ah yes, make him squirm," he winked.

CHAPTER
NINETEEN

Until I return. Kelly lay on her bed reading the note Theo had left for what must have been the hundredth time. Fiddling with the edges, she let out a bored sigh, then dived into the bottom of her bag and retrieved her phone. She powered it on and waited for the display to load. *4:03 a.m. Is it too early for vampires? Eh, who cares? I need to talk to Theo, and I have got to get out of this room.* She tossed her phone back into her bag and switched her track pants for jeans, slipped on her sneakers and pulled on her sweatshirt.

Reaching for the doorknob, she hesitated, listening for movement in the hall. After a moment, she slipped out of her room, glancing down the hall in both directions. Empty. Tucking her hands into her pockets, she made her way through the atrium.

She studied a directory on the wall, scanning all the wings and offices; one grabbed her attention, the Office of Vampire Affairs. *Fabian. Theo must be with him.* Kelly headed off toward Fabian's office. As she reached the end of the hall on the opposite end, a sliver of light sliced through the darkness.

"We cannot sit ideally by," a woman's voice said.

"Your concerns do not fall on deaf ears. They simply need further investigation," a man responded in a calm, dulcet tone.

"Further investigation? I have given you everything you need."

Kelly made her way toward the door. Every delicate step she took felt like a thundering stomp. She peeked into the crack; the woman's blonde hair danced across the black laces of her intricate purple corset that accentuated her familiar curves as she paced in front of a large ornate desk while the man seated behind it faced a warm flickering light.

"After recent events, there is a higher level of apprehension on me. I cannot blindly agree to situations that could jeopardize the standings of the court or the council," he reasoned.

"So, you will do nothing?" the woman spat. *Her voice, why is it familiar?*

He turned to face the woman. "There are other avenues that need exploration before your solution is an option."

"The longer you and your puppets sit on their hands, the more our family dies."

"You will watch your tone with me. I need not remind you why I was placed in charge of our people," he said, getting to his feet, placing his fingertips on the desk as he leaned forward. He reminded her of a lion ready to pounce. The woman went rigid, then spun on her heel, heading for the door. Kelly raised her fist as if she was about to knock when the door was wrenched open. Gabriella stood, lips pressed as she glared at her. Her lip twisted to a sneer at the sight of her. Kelly's heart rammed against her chest, waiting for Gabriella to make the first move.

"We will continue this later," Fabian called as Gabriella pushed past Kelly, disappearing into the darkened hall.

"You must be the illustrious Ms. Frost. Please, come in." He straightened up, adjusting his waistcoat.

The vastness of his office was emphasized by an ornately designed redwood and walnut floor that blended into the sophisticated black and crimson damask walls. Large paintings and antique sconces that encumbered the majority of the room were lit by a fire burning in the imposing grand fireplace. The farther she entered, the more detailed and immense the room became. Behind the desk, a wrought-iron railing separated the balcony from the room below.

"Are you Fabian?"

"I am. Please, sit?" He smiled, gesturing to the chair opposite him to be welcoming. If it weren't for his fangs, she may have believed it. "How may I be of service?"

Kelly hesitated, standing next to the chair, gaze raking over the man in front of her. If there was a stereotype for vampires, he was it. Dressed in all black, from his classic long hair to the elegant waistcoat covering a puffy black shirt. Screaming in contrast to his pallid complexion, the only bits of color being the dark circles under his eyes, his eerily pink lips, and a small ruby in the center of the silver bat broach on his chest. He wore several silver rings on each hand, along with one fashioned into a claw on his thumb. A small chill ran down her back as the image of a porcelain doll flicked through her mind. Fabian stepped out from behind his desk, leisurely drifting toward her. Her muscles tensed, ready to defend herself if the time came. *Stay calm.*

"Are those for intimidation or just fashion?" she asked,

hiding her uneasiness with criticism.

He paused behind her. "What do you think?"

"It can't be real silver, therefore it has to be fashion."

"Is that so?" Kelly's hair shifted as he lifted a few strands and let them fall from his fingers.

"If it was, you would have serious burns anywhere it touched," she replied, trying to maintain her poise.

"Indeed, however, I have found steel works just as well to get the point across." His sophisticated demeanor didn't stop the words from slithering down her spine.

She took a half step away from him. "Is Theo here? I need to speak with him."

"He was here. He informed me about your meeting and the unfortunate entanglement with Alexander. I couldn't help but wonder why either of them would waste their time and energy on some human. But now meeting you in person—" He returned to his seat, resting his fingertips together. "—you are not *some* human. You're rather unique. Not only did you slaughter a room full of my kin, but you emerged unscathed. Tell me, how is that possible?"

"Just because you can't see the scars doesn't mean they aren't there." Her voice caught in her throat.

"What's still puzzling me is why Alexander wanted you in the first place?" he asked, crossing to the small bar cart next to the fireplace.

"I don't know. You'd have to ask him," she said sardonically. "You said Theo *was* here. As in past tense."

"That is correct."

"Do you know where he is?"

"Possibly," he said, taking a sip from his glass goblet. Kelly watched the blood cling to the side.

"It's a yes or no question."

"My knowledge of his physical location is dependent on

your cooperation."

"What do you want?" she asked, burying her apprehension and annoyance.

"Nothing at the moment, just your word that if I require your *unique* talents, you will come to my aide no questions asked."

"Why would I do that?"

"Because you did not massacre that room alone. For a vampire to kill one of its own kind without prior authorization is a severe violation of our customs."

"It was self-defense," she argued.

"There is no such thing in our world."

"The council—"

"There are cases that do not require the council's attention."

"If I don't?" she challenged.

"Mr. Walsh may not see the light of day, so to speak," he smiled. Showing his fangs as a subtle reminder of the power he possessed.

"Fine, I'll do it," she grumbled.

Fabian held out his hand. "It is not an understanding until it's shaken upon." Kelly hesitated, then clasped his hand. It was like touching dry ice. Pain shot through her hand as he gripped it. The silver claw on his thumb dug into the back of her hand. She clenched her jaw to ignore the pain until he released. A thin trickle of blood inched down her hand.

"Theo is running an errand; he should return later today."

"Thank you," she said through gritted teeth.

"Until we meet again," he said with a nod and sinister air in his voice.

Fuck.

CHAPTER
TWENTY

Kelly stared at the ceiling of her room, waiting for the world to wake and planning how she would handle the situations with Jonas and Theo. *First, I will handle Jonas, then when that is taken care of and he's back, I can talk to Theo and find out why he lied.* She showered and dressed, then bounded out of her room with determination. Accidentally walking into the petite nurse that was always sent to retrieve her.

"Ouch," the nurse exclaimed. A flurry of papers falling around them.

"Oh, I'm sorry, I'm in my own world," Kelly apologized, helping her retrieve the scattered papers.

"It's fine. I wasn't paying attention either."

"I never got your name," Kelly said, getting to her feet and handing the nurse back her paperwork.

"Gaia, Gaia Shade."

"Nice to meet you, Gaia. I'm Kelly. Sorry again." Kelly gave her an apologetic smile. Gaia returned it and stepped past her. As her footsteps faded, Kelly spun on her heel.

"Hey, Gaia, have you seen Jonas or Theo?" Kelly called.

Gaia turned around and looked at her, puzzled by Theo's name. "Theo Walsh, he's a vampire, er, big, looks like an eighties heartthrob." Kelly held up her hand at his estimated height.

"No, sorry, but Jonas should be at home."

"Okay, thanks."

The route to Jonas's house now passed in a second. She paused as she reached for the doorknob. *Don't let him get to you. Calm and collected.* Taking a deep, steading breath, she pushed the door open. The early morning silence carried the sound of clinking mugs and a kettle being put on the stove through the house. She cut through the room stacked with books into the kitchen. Jonas cleared his throat several times and shrugged, pulling his wool cardigan tighter around him.

"Are you sick?" Kelly asked. Jonas glanced over at her.

"It's nothing, a bit below par this morning, that's all," he said, pulling out tea and honey from the cabinet.

"Go sit. I'll bring it in when it's ready," Kelly sighed, setting aside her frustration with him for the moment. If there was one thing she knew as fact it was: Frosts are always stubborn as a mule when they're not feeling well, they don't like being coddled and they will not ask for help.

"I am perfectly capable of making my own tea," he muttered, fumbling with the jar of honey. Kelly lurched forward, catching it before it hit the floor.

"Go. Now," she commanded.

His determined glare softened as he stepped past her and headed for his study. A few moments later, the kettle whistled. She turned off the flame, poured the water into the intricate painted blue and white teapot, prepared the matching serving platter with a cup, honey and a small cream jug, then carried it all into the study.

Jonas was standing in front of a small end table when she entered. He tucked a small vial containing a shimmering blue liquid into his pocket, then returned to his desk, surrounded by his usual stack of books and old papers. The corner had been cleared just big enough for the tray. She poured some tea into the cup, then sat across from him.

"Thank you," he mumbled, adding a bit of honey, then taking the cup from the tray.

"You're welcome," she replied. They sat quietly for a moment while Jonas sipped the tea. *He looks tired and pale. Maybe now isn't the best time. Or maybe he will be more agreeable.*

"We need to get things straightened out," Kelly said sternly.

"Indeed, what you said during your tantrum yesterday has not gone unheard. However, there is something far more important we need to discuss first. Before your training with Ms. Kazem, when I touched your arm, you said you saw children under a Christmas tree. I need you to elaborate on what you saw." He cleared his throat and readied a pen and piece of paper.

"Er... okay. Like I said, there were three children. I think the oldest girl was eight, maybe ten years old, then a boy, and the youngest was another girl."

"What can you tell me about them?" Jonas asked, leaning forward in his chair.

"They all looked related, brown hair, fair skin, nicely dressed, I think. Their clothes were old-fashioned, but they looked clean, like church clothes or something. They were outside at first, running around like they were flying a kite or maybe playing tag." She closed her eyes tight, trying to remember everything she had seen.

"What else?"

"One of them shouted, I think it was the other name. Amelia... Emma... Emily, I think, I can't be sure."

Jonas leaned back in his chair, touching his fingertips together and pressing them to his lips, his eyebrows knit, lost in thought.

"What is it?"

"Something remarkable. This must be a new ability for conduits. You were able to see my past, my childhood. Those children were my siblings." Jonas had gotten to his feet and begun pacing back and forth.

"You saw it too, then?"

"No." Jonas stopped to stare out the large window into the back garden. His back to Kelly. "I saw patches of tan, large black guns and concrete walls. I saw a white-tiled room covered in blood. So much blood." The room fell silent.

"What I saw were only glimpses, like a photograph, and there was no sound or smells. I have searched through all of my books, but as far as I have found, this situation, this connection, has never happened before."

"What does that mean, then?"

"I'm not sure, but I do owe you an apology. I have been kept away from the modern world for my safety. As a result, I was blind to the customs that have emerged in the time since." He bowed his head, and returning to his desk, locked eyes with her. "I can only try to do better, but it will take time. Can you accept my apology?" he asked, his genuine tone catching her off guard.

"On one condition." Her voice was gentle.

"That is?"

"What happened between you and Theo?"

Jonas fell silent again, a solemn look crossed his face. He handed her the picture frame from the center of the desk and sat. Kelly took it. The photo was of a handsome gentleman standing behind his beautiful wife, seated with a child on her lap and three more standing around her. She recognized the children as Jonas's siblings, only a few years younger.

"The girl standing on the right is my sister, Emily." He stopped as if the very thought tore at his soul. "They met at a Christmas party in 1868."

"She is *his* Emily, his wife, that—" Kelly stammered, now staring in shock at the photo as all the pieces fell into place. Jonas was Theo's brother-in-law. He had been so distraught when Emily died, he abandoned everything. "You blame him for her death, don't you?"

"Yes."

"It wasn't Theo, it was Alexander," she said, glancing up at him, confusion written on his face. "He was jealous. He said that he had *seen* her first," Kelly explained.

"How do you know this?"

"Alexander bragged to Theo while he was trying to rescue me. He drained her until she was too weak. Then once she died, Alexander wanted to make Theo suffer more and followed him to Paris and made him his slave. He didn't tell you this?"

"I didn't see him until his trial. I was so filled with hate that I refused to speak with him."

A far-off look accompanied the pained expression written on his face as a heavy silence fell between them.

Two voices filled the hall, followed by the distant thump of the front door closing. A moment later, Eli and Wyatt entered the study talking animatedly about an after-party of some kind.

"And that's when Jimmy crashed headfirst through the door," Wyatt laughed.

"Wyatt? Eli? What are you guys doing here?"

"Oh hey, Kelly. I told you last night, Jonas is my new boss. I need to check in," Eli said brightly.

"Same here, well he's not my new boss, just my boss," Wyatt added.

"What do you have to report, Wyatt?"

"About twelve missing persons out of the greater London area," he said, the lighthearted expression he had entered with vanished.

"Human?" Jonas asked before taking another sip of tea.

"From what I could find out, only four were human; seven were werewolves and one fae." Wyatt handed a file to him. Jonas examined the contents.

"All from the Leak Street area?"

"Within a few miles at least, the bartender at Delirium remembers a few of them visiting around the time they disappeared."

"Head to Los Angeles, there has been rumors of an increase in missing persons. Report back with your findings." Jonas closed the file, adding it to the pile of papers on his desk.

"You got it, boss. Great to see you, Kelly. Let Theo know I'll catch him later," Wyatt said, heading out of the office.

"You are?" Jonas asked, turning his attention to Eli, who was idly looking around the room.

"Eli Palmer, it's great to officially meet you, sir." Eli handed him a file similar to Wyatt's. Jonas flipped through the first few pages.

"What is an E.M.T?"

"Emergency medical technician," Eli answered.

"I'm afraid I'm not familiar with the term."

"Traveling doctor," Kelly answered.

"To an extent," Eli finished.

"Do have any combat experience?" Jonas asked.

"No, not technically. The only combat I was in was at Alexander's mansion."

"It says here 'scout.' Can you elaborate?"

"Autumn made me this so that I could find people that may need our help. It helped me find Kelly," he said, removing his pendant from under his shirt.

"Do you trust him?" Jonas directed the question to Kelly.

"With my life," she stated, unwavering.

"You will need combat training. Report to Doctor William Dakota for a physical, then to the athletics center."

"Thank you," Eli said, then winked at Kelly and left.

"What *do* you do?" she asked. Jonas grabbed a handkerchief from his pocket and stifled a cough.

"I am in charge of law enforcement for the council. Unfortunately, there are only a handful of enforcers, so we can only go after the bigger offenders, the ones that threaten to expose us to the human world."

"What about me?"

"I am still working on that; I suppose after extensive training, I may put you in the field with a partner."

"Extensive training?" Kelly echoed. Jonas shot her a look. "What do you mean by extensive?" she clarified.

"We need to discover and hone all your supernatural abilities as well as your combative ones."

"That could take years!" Kelly exclaimed.

"In addition to figuring out any other new conduit-related abilities that may present themselves. You need to learn how to fight fae, vampires, shifters, and werewolves," Jonas continued.

"Can't you just shoot them with silver bullets?"

"From what I have been told, that is entirely, er, Hollywood. Besides, the price of silver has skyrocketed. It would be far too expensive."

"What do you mean 'from what you have been told?'"

"I was told of these films—"

"Wait, stop, hold the phone. You have never seen a movie? Ever?"

"No, and frankly I am baffled by the fascination," Jonas said as he shuffled papers and books around his desk. He then headed down the hall.

"Wait till you hear about the internet," Kelly mumbled.

"Are you coming?" he called, swapping his sweater for a jacket.

Kelly bolted out of her seat and tore off after him.

"Are you sure you don't want to get some rest?"

"We will never get anywhere resting on our laurels."

"You said I have abilities. You mean more than just the shield and whatever happened during my session with Evalyn?"

"Yes, as I told you before, the conduit's purpose is to protect the human world from the supernatural and the supernatural from the human. I know of several abilities that a conduit possesses of their own power, but there are the abilities they can channel."

"Channel? What do you mean?"

"We really must work on your parroting. For a shapeshifter, with a little assistance, you would be able to shift from human to a form of animal, much like they can, with it, you would have their same heightened senses and reflexes."

Before Kelly realized, they were pushing open the door

to the athletics center. Evalyn was sitting on the floor in the same position as before.

"We need to work on offensive training, which should, in part, strengthen your defense. You did produce a shield, but it was little more than padded leather. Take your position again," he said, pointing in Evalyn's direction as he took a seat in the metal chair and readied his note pad.

CHAPTER
TWENTY-ONE

After a couple more hours of practice, she could effortlessly maintain her shield. Jonas had taken to distracting Kelly from one side while Evelyn attacked from another until it became second nature. He sat in the metal chair, jotting notes in his portfolio. Kelly lay stretched out on the floor staring up at the ceiling, letting her lunch settle while waiting to start the next part of her training. Kelly thought back to everything they had discussed that morning, remembering his family photo. Emily's perfect curls and the last remaining bit of baby fat in her cheeks she would soon grow out of.

"What were they like?"

"What were who like?" Jonas answered, still scribbling notes.

"Your siblings?" she asked, sitting up and facing him. He glanced over his glasses.

"They were like any other siblings; they had their moments of kindness and their moments of annoyance. I was the eldest, Emily was next, she was three years younger than I, then there was Bran, who was four years younger, and Margaret, she was the baby, six years younger."

The door swung open. Billy entered wearing a gray sweatshirt and some track pants, followed closely by Eli. Billy handed Jonas a folder. Jonas flipped through it. Kelly sneezed.

"Well, that's something you don't see every day," he mumbled.

"What?" Eli asked, a hint of worry in his voice.

"One hundred percent human, no magical properties at all." Jonas placed the folder in his portfolio and stood. "Are you ready?" He directed the question at Billy.

"Absolutely." Billy began undressing, removing his sweatshirt and white tank top, revealing his muscular physique. Kelly had forgotten just how fit he was. He took off his sneakers, track pants, and was left only in his boxer briefs. She caught herself staring and turned her attention to the space on the floor in front of her. He started stretching by rolling his head, extending his neck, and swinging his arms. Then nodded at Jonas.

"On your feet, Frost," Billy quipped.

"What's going on?" she asked Jonas, getting to her feet.

"Billy is going to help you with the next bit of training."

"And he has to be naked for that?"

"Not naked," Eli chimed.

"How's he supposed to help? He's a doctor. Unless he's going to show me the weakest points to hit."

"Stomp the toes and blind them!" Eli exclaimed. They all paused, staring at him. "Not permanently, just, like, poke their eye or throw sand in the face."

"Go ahead, Doctor, Eli, stand over here," Jonas said, gesturing toward the metal chair away from where Billy was standing. Billy took a few steps back. Kelly watched in amazement as the bones in his hand broke and reformed. He dropped to all fours as his tawny skin transformed into golden brown fur, a long tail sprouted from his backside. He placed his head on the floor as each of his ribs violently cracked and shifted.

The edges of his ears stretched and twisted. He took a few heaving breaths, then lifted his head off the floor. His dark eyes were now large and golden, fur covered every inch of him. Kelly stood in shock as she stared at the large mountain cat that had been her ex-boyfriend. She slowly circled him, dumbfounded, trying to take in what she had witnessed. She knelt in front of him as he sat up, and she lowered her head level with his. Looking deep in his eyes, she saw past the feline shell and to the human waiting inside.

"Did it hurt?" she asked. The cougar shook its head.

"Doctor Dakota is our resident shifter and has offered to teach you how to fight them," Jonas clarified.

"I guess that explains why I always used to sneeze around you."

"Wait, are shifters different animals?" Eli asked.

"Of course. Shifters are merely the classification, but we will get into that later. For now, we will show how shapeshifting is imperative for the conduit in battle and establish a baseline," Jonas said. "Do not be fooled by the beast before you. Though natural cougars are typically reclusive and only attack when threatened, shifters are still human. Therefore, most shifters fight the same as well as have strategic knowledge."

Kelly and Billy stood facing each other in the center of the room. There a decent amount of space between them. He paced back and forth, and Kelly tensed her muscles, ready to react at any moment. Billy suddenly growled menacingly before stopping, dropping low, and jumping toward Kelly. She swiftly lunged to the left, falling hard onto the wooden floor as Billy fiercely landed on top of her. Using his paws, he pinned her to the ground and snarled while nipping at her. Kelly slid her arm beneath Billy's chest and grabbed his throat, feeling for his windpipe under the thick fur. Billy writhed and squirmed to free himself from her grasp. Kelly then got her knee under him and pushed him away with all her might, only to have him land a foot away. Billy stood up. Kelly scrambled to her feet, ready for another attack if necessary.

"Good, now drink this, and try again," Jonas said, removing the small glass vial from his pocket.

"What is it?" Kelly asked.

"Just drink it," Jonas sighed.

Kelly popped the small cork, releasing the potent stench of rotten meat and wild animal dander. She cringed, then swallowed the contents in a single gulp. Her skin erupted with goose bumps, then an icy-hot fire spread throughout her body like lava consuming every inch of her.

"You can fight the change and harness the animal's abilities, or you can shift like Billy and fight that way. You only need to focus," Jonas said, his voice distant.

The muscles in her back contorted painfully, twisting inside out as if they had been put in a roaring furnace. She let out an agonized scream, but out came an aggressive growl.

As the torturous pain subsided, she opened her eyes. Sitting up, her head spun, blurring her vision. *Something is wrong. No, not wrong, just off.* As her vision cleared, she glanced down. Her legs had grown twice their size and were distorted, bending at weird angles. Raising a hand to rub her face, she gasped at what she saw: long razor-sharp claws instead of fingers, and her entire body morphed into something unrecognizable. Panic rushed through her veins as she glanced at Jonas. Out of the corner of her eye, Eli darted from the room. Getting to her feet, she pawed her face. Her heart hammered in her chest as panic overwhelmed her.

"Kelly, Kelly, over here." Eli's voice echoed like an explosion in a cave. Kelly clasped her hands over her ears. Jonas grabbed Eli then holding his finger to his lips.

"Quietly," Jonas said in a whisper, but to Kelly's heightened senses it sounded normal.

"Sorry, I grabbed this for you," Eli whispered, propping a large mirror against his legs. Kelly crouched, taking in her new form. She was something unrecognizable; her nose and mouth had stretched and twisted to become more snout-like, her ears now pointed and pinned back. An image of her dog, Thor, flicked through her mind. Her new, more muscular, and rigid form had forced her clothes to their limits and were now clinging to her like a second skin. The leather bracelet Autumn had given her was uncomfortably tight on her wrist. Her skin had adapted to the would-be patterns and color patches of dark smoky gray and black, instead of sprouting animal-like fur.

"How do you feel?" Jonas whispered. Kelly went to speak, but all that came out was a doglike whine. "Yes, I suppose you should be a bit apprehensive and possibly confused."

Kelly carefully shifted her weight. It was like being a child learning how to walk. Wobbling and stumbling, she took one step, then another. She paced back and forth for a minute, getting acclimated to her new form.

Eli's muscles tensed, not enough that a person would see. To Kelly, it was as if he was in full defense mode. She leaned back on her haunches. A small whimper escaped her chest.

"I'm not scared of you, you're just a lot bigger," Eli said, trying to comfort her. He held out his hand. Almost reflexively, she bowed her head, allowing him to place his hand on her head.

"Good girl," Eli joked. Kelly playfully nipped at him, then held out her wrist. Eli removed the bracelet and put it in his pocket.

"Are you ready?"

Kelly nodded.

"Let's get back to work," Jonas said.

She cocked her head, staring at him. There was something different about him. She sniffed. The surrounding air was a mixture of protective father and mesmerized scientist. It filled her head with more questions than before. Blowing a quick burst of air from her nose, trying to remove the scent, she regained her focus.

Moving back to her spot on the floor. Billy returned to his feet, waiting for Kelly to signal she was ready. Her eyes connected with Billy's; a primal surge coursed through her. Billy darted forward, leaping into the air. Kelly froze. She may have contempt for him, but didn't want to see him injured. *How am I supposed to fight without seriously hurting him?* She threw her hands up just in time. Billy's body slammed into hers, hurtling them both to the ground. As she hit the floor, Billy continued sliding a few feet away. He was on his feet in a second and attacked again. Kelly scrambled to her feet only to be slammed face-first back to the floor. She rolled, knocking Billy away. He recovered and attacked again, this time pinning her to the floor as she struggled against his weight. He snarled his long yellow teeth at her. *Not again.* She reached her arms under his chest, lifting him off of her and tossing him. Sharp pain shot through her forearm. Billy landed several feet away. Kelly turned onto her side, her skin feeling as though it was crawling with a thousand tiny legs. She took a deep breath, feeling the weight of her transformed body slowly shrinking back to its original form. She could hear her heavy breathing, the sound loud in her ears. The air was thick with the smell of sweat and the musky odor of the creature she had just become. As her body returned to normal, she could feel her muscles relaxing and her heartbeat slowed. The sensation was both painful and relief at the same time. Her muscles were heavy and prickled, as if every limb had fallen asleep.

Billy walked casually back over to Jonas and Eli, shifting in three steps back to his human form.

"Why did you change back?" she asked.

"You're bleeding," he said, removing a small first aid kit from his pile of clothes. Sitting up, Kelly glanced at her arm. When she had launched him across the room, his claws dug into her forearm. She twisted her arm around for a better look. Four parallel lines curved down the outside of her forearm. Billy dabbed at the blood. The cuts were already beginning to heal.

"It's fine, see. Just a scratch," she said coldly.

"Part of your conduit abilities is accelerated healing, not faster than say a vampire but definitely faster than a human, and possibly faster than a shifter but hard to tell at the moment," Jonas commented as Billy wiped away the final bit of blood from her arm. He looked up at her with an apologetic expression.

"You can stop now," Kelly sneered. Her anger at her poor fighting skills mixing with the years of hurt forced her to hold back the million other things she wanted to say. Billy closed the first aid kit and got to his feet.

"I need to get back to the office. I can do another session tomorrow. If you need anything, you know where to find me," he said to Jonas as he slipped back into his clothes. He shot a hurt glare at Kelly, then pushed the door open, passing Wyatt heading in.

CHAPTER
TWENTY-TWO

"Hey there, Billy boy, how's it hanging?" Wyatt said, to no response. "Jee wiz, what climbed in his jockey shorts?"

"I thought you were going to LA?" Kelly asked, resting her arms on her knees, running her hand across her head.

"My flight isn't until tomorrow. Heard the party was happening in here. Thought I'd swing by."

"Perfect. Would you be up for a sparring match?" Jonas asked.

"Sparring?" Kelly asked.

"Sure, sounds good. Thought you were out of the game?" Wyatt asked, as he bounced back and forth on his toes, throwing a fake jab at him.

"I will not be your opponent, Kelly will," Jonas said.

"Oh nice, want me to go easy on you?" Wyatt joked.

"Is there a problem?" Jonas looked at her puzzled face and asked.

"I thought we were done for the day," she said, wiping

162

the sweat from her forehead. *I need a break, a minute to breathe.*

"Technically. We need to wait until after sunset," Jonas said.

"Why?"

"The sun may not make us burst into flame, but it puts a damper on our strength. We are nearly five times stronger at night," Wyatt answered.

"But at Alexander's—"

"Your unique situation seems to have created a torrent of suppressed power that all surfaced at once," Jonas explained. Kelly stared at him blankly.

"From the stories I have heard, it's similar to a dam breaking, sending your magic gauge from zero to one hundred in no time flat," Wyatt commented. Kelly's sharp glance made Eli look away and examine another area of the room.

"I suppose that is accurate, crude but accurate. Now that your powers have leveled out, it will be a typical fight, but more challenging than you are accustomed to," Jonas continued.

"That makes sense, I guess, but I thought Theo would continue training me on how to fight vampires?" Kelly asked, getting to her feet.

"He is still on business in the Black Forest," Wyatt said.

"Besides, it is beneficial to fight against someone that will not go easy on you," Jonas interjected.

"Then why did I just fight Billy? Is that what you call going easy?" Kelly said, getting to her feet.

"Yes, you have had no prior shifter training, so today was a bit of a crash course. Whereas you have an elementary knowledge of vampire combat, I fear if you were to spar against Theo you wouldn't improve or learn to properly defend yourself," Jonas stated.

"When will he be back?" Kelly asked.

"No idea. Shouldn't be more than a day." Wyatt shrugged.

"And wouldn't it be great to kick Theo's butt next time he pisses you off?" With a laugh, Eli tossed her a towel and her bracelet.

"I guess," she sighed, catching each.

"Best study up. It will only become more challenging from here on out. Be back at 10 p.m. on the dot. Eli, you're with me," Jonas instructed, slipping on his jacket as he left Eli on his heel.

"Nice. That gives me enough time to get my drink on," Wyatt said with enthusiasm.

"You're going to fight me drunk? Is that wise?" she asked, wiping the sweat and the remaining traces of blood from her arm.

"That would be entertaining and probably give you a slight advantage, but not what I meant."

"Oh." She stopped as his real meaning clicked in her head.

"I'll catch ya later. Don't forget to bring your A-game 'cause I won't be going easy on you," he said as the doors swung shut behind them and he continued toward the atrium.

Kelly entered her room to find a stack of books on her bed. She let out an exhausted sigh. She tossed her bracelet onto her bed and examined a few covers. They were worn and outdated by at least three decades. *After.*

Nearly falling asleep in the shower from the relaxing heat, she struggled to get dressed. Every muscle felt drained of any remaining strength. A throbbing pang coursed through her jaw, creeping its way up the side of her face. *Did I bring painkillers? Maybe I'll take a nap before studying.* Her mind wandered as she grabbed her hairbrush. A dull aching pressure radiated up her arm as if it was tangled in something. She examined her forearm. Nothing. No deep cuts, no raised skin, only the slightest silver lines from Billy's claws. *Probably just sore like the rest of me.* She grabbed the brush again, this time with her other hand. The dull pressure mirroring the other.

"What the fuck?" she whispered, dropping her brush. Holding her forearms together, she stared at them. Each arm was circled with a wide, faint brownish-yellow tinge, resembling a week-old bruise, from wrist to elbow. *Not again. God, please no.* As she stared at each arm, she could barely make out the odd wavy outline. *I need to find Autumn.* Panic sent her heart racing and with it all the memories of Alexander invading her dreams and the darkness that left her with unexplainable bruises. *Hold your horses there, worry wart. You just got done fighting. It's probably nothing and will fade in a day or so. It's not even an actual bruise or anything. Just throw on a long-sleeve shirt or sweatshirt. You're fine.*

She took several deep, steadying breaths, regaining her composure, locking eyes with her reflection.

"I'm fine. Everything is fine," she lied. Turning away from the truth, staring back at her and at the mountain of homework.

~

ENTERING THE ATHLETICS CENTER, she spotted Jonas, Eli, and Wyatt already in the middle of the room. She stretched, hoping to lessen the ache still coursing through her. She wandered in circles for a minute, swinging her arms forward and back, to one side, then the other. Stretching as much as she could.

"You ready for an ass whooping?" Wyatt taunted with an air of humor in his voice.

"Bring it on, old man," she replied. "Oh, I should probably take these off. I don't want it to hurt you." She removed the pendant from her neck and gave it to Eli. He slipped it into his pocket. Wyatt slid off his jacket and tossed it over to Jonas.

They faced each other, standing a few feet apart. They studied each other for signs of weakness, searching for an opportunity to strike. A wrenching pain shot through her stomach suddenly, making her double over. Gritting her teeth, she ignored it. *It's nothing.* She straightened up and readied herself again. Suddenly gasping for breath like the wind had been knocked out of her, she dropped to all fours. *Was this Wyatt? How was he doing that?* Burning pain shot through her forearms. Jonas, Eli, and Wyatt all rushed around her.

"Are you alright?" Eli said.

"I didn't do anything!" Wyatt exclaimed.

"It could be a delayed side effect of the shapeshifter potion," Jonas commented.

"Here, drink this." Jonas handed her another small glass vial. This one she recognized from her lesson in potion making with Autumn. *Don't swish.* Kelly popped the cork and swallowed it in a single gulp. The mint and lemon filled her senses. *So that's what it's supposed to taste like.* Her breathing returned to normal, and the pain became a dull, sore throb.

"Side effect?" she asked, looking up at Jonas.

"I can't be sure. I haven't had the chance to properly

test it. It may need a few more adjustments for your stature," he said, jotting notes in his portfolio.

"You gave me an untested potion," Kelly shouted.

"You drank it," Eli commented. She shot a glare at him.

"How did you know it wasn't going to kill me?" she barked.

"I have done my research," Jonas said stiffly.

"Clearly you missed something."

"We don't have to fight," Wyatt tried to reassure her.

"No, it's fine, just give me a minute," Kelly said, taking a few deep breaths, then returning to her feet. "I'm good. Let's do this."

"If you're certain you are alright. I will return to my study. Maybe I can formulate a solution for any other side effects, if it was in fact a side effect of your transformation," Jonas said, signaling again for Eli to follow.

"I won't go too hard on you," Wyatt said, his face illuminated by a mischievous grin. Kelly watched as he dashed away from her, leaving a blurred trail of movement behind him. She smirked. He had no idea she could follow his movements. He swung at her; she moved just enough for him to miss and she responded with a punch of her own. She readied herself for the next attack, both of them moving around the room. His fist flew toward her face, almost missing her ear as she ducked away. Then she sprang up and used all her strength to lunge into him, pushing him backward. He recovered and struck out again, but she dodged or block every hit. The memories of her training with Theo came back in a wave of calm. Every frustration, every question that remained unanswered, silenced. They continued to maneuver around the room until Kelly unleashed a kick that sent Wyatt sprawling onto the floor. Both exhausted, they looked at each other and knew the fight was done; Kelly had won. Wyatt lay there panting while Kelly stood above him, feeling an immense sense of accomplishment. He smiled upward at her and said in a raspy voice, "Damn, you're good."

"Theo's an excellent teacher," Kelly said, wishing he was here instead of Wyatt.

CHAPTER
TWENTY-THREE

Kelly tossed and turned in her bed, her mind racing. *Where is Theo? He should have returned by now.* The familiar pang of guilt weighing heavy in her chest. *I need to talk to him.* With a heavy sigh, she rolled onto her side. A wave of sore muscles greeted her. *Something isn't right. Why do I hurt so much? Even without the health potion. I healed so quickly after Alexander's and after the match with Billy. Why is now any different? Is there something about fighting Wyatt?* Unable to bear the pain any longer, Kelly got up, wincing as a powerful jolt shot through the tattoo-like mark on her forearm. *What the fuck?* She threw open the door, determined to get some answers.

"Kelly!" Billy called from the hall. "I just got off the phone with Jonas. He wants to see us."

He's like a bad fucking penny. "Did he say why or what for?" she grumbled.

"Nope, just to get you and head over immediately," Billy said.

"Fine. Let's go," she said, blowing past him.

They walked in silence to Jonas's, Billy two steps behind

her. The street was still dark, the morning light slowly taking over. Light poured through the narrow gaps between drawn curtains. She barged into the house, heading straight back to the study. It took a minute to realize Jonas wasn't hidden behind the stacks of books on his desk like he normally was. She went to the kitchen, not there, then the front room.

"Where is he?" she asked, more to herself than Billy. "Jonas, Jonas!" she bellowed without waiting for an answer. A lump formed in her throat. *Did something happen? Is he okay?*

"Stop yelling, I'm up here," Jonas yelled from above. Kelly sprinted up the stairs, taking them two at a time, pausing for a moment on the landing. The rooms at either end of the hallway were draped in shadows. A faint light was emanating from the central room.

The walls were exact copies of the walls downstairs. Like a library of the past, every wall and surface piled high with books, newspapers, folders with papers dangling haphazardly from them. She cautiously stepped further into the room, aware that a single misstep could easily cause an avalanche of books. A long table in the center of the room was stacked with books open to different pages and loose scraps of paper scattered about. Jonas sat in the corner of the room; his distinguished features seemed more ragged. Dark circles punctuated his striking blue eyes, his beard was grayer and scragglier. He was wrapped in his dark gray cable-knit cardigan with a blanket draped over his legs. A large tome rested in his lap, its pages rustling as he turned them. He looked up from the text before him.

"Good, now I need you to run an errand." His voice became raspy and strained as he talked. Kelly carefully weaved through the room over to him.

"At four in the morning? It couldn't wait until later? Like when people are actually awake?" Kelly asked.

"No, it can't. The flight leaves in a couple hours." He tugged on the lapel of his sweater.

"Flight? What flight? You said errand, what kind of errand requires air travel?"

"One of the utmost importance," he said before beginning to cough violently.

"Are you alright?" Billy asked, rushing to his side.

"I'm fine, I'm fine," Jonas snapped, brushing him away.

"I'll get you a glass of water," Billy said, leaving the room.

"You lied. This isn't nothing, you *are* getting sick. You need rest. We can talk about this later," Kelly said, turning for the door.

"No, there isn't time," he barked. Kelly stopped, then took a deep, steadying breath.

"If I do your errand, will you get some rest? Proper rest?" she asked through partly gritted teeth.

"Fine," he agreed grudgingly.

Kelly exhaled heavily and asked, "Alright, where do I have to go?"

He waved toward her and Billy, who was now holding a cup of water just outside the door. "You both are going," he said.

"I think I can handle whatever it is on my own. Just tell me what I am doing and where I am going."

"It's not up for debate, you are not going alone," Jonas said.

"What about Eli? Why can't he go with me?" she asked.

"He is busy with other matters; Doctor Dakota is going. End of discussion." His commanding tone that Kelly had thought gone returned. Billy handed the glass of water to Jonas.

"Where are *we* going?" She groaned.

"To the birthplace of the first conduit," Jonas said after taking a few sips from the glass. Kelly looked at him in confusion. He gestured to the stool behind her. She grabbed it and pulled it alongside him.

"There is a legend that has been passed down through the conduit line," he began. Kelly glanced at Billy. "The legend is of a cage or prison that the supernatural creatures escaped from many centuries ago. A woman claimed to hear voices coming from the cage, begging for help and promising that all her wishes would come true if only she opened it. When she did, the monsters escaped into the world. Once she realized what she had done, she tried to close it, but it was too late. Legend says that the demons themselves were the only ones that didn't escape."

"Wait, this sounds familiar." Billy's voice was soft but questioning, a gentle wave of confusion and curiosity.

"It sounds like the myth of Pandora's box." Kelly spoke in a low, thoughtful tone, as the realization settled in.

"Ultimately, the story you know concludes with a lesson on why evil exists in our world. The legend actually continues. The monsters set free scattered to the corners of the world, wreaking chaos and mayhem everywhere they went, turning the earth into their own blood-soaked playground. After years of failed attempts and lost battles, a person able to wield the earth's natural magic discovered a woman with child who had been attacked, she clung to life begging for help. The Arch-Magi was able to cure her, but it forever changed the child and unknowingly any descendant of that child."

"That was the first conduit?" Kelly asked intently.

"Yes, that was our beginning, and we have since sought to protect those who cannot see the world as we do and protect themselves. All while searching for the cage that can contain the evils once again."

"What does this have to do with the errand?" Billy posed.

"Ever since the monsters were released, the conduits have made it their priority to locate both the cage and its key, with occasional help from the council," Jonas informed them.

"There is a key?" Kelly asked.

"Assuming I haven't misinterpreted any of the documents, yes, though what form it and the cage takes is still unknown."

"It's a key, right? Everyone knows what a key looks like," Billy said.

"Keys aren't always just a piece of jagged metal. A key is merely a way of completing a puzzle that opens a lock," Jonas corrected.

"And I'm guessing we don't know where the cage is, so we can't reverse engineer its image?"

"That would be accurate. I'm still trying to narrow down the location of the cage, but I think I have an idea of where the key might be." Jonas's voice grew strained as he took a sip of water from his glass.

"Which is the errand, right?" Kelly asked. Jonas nodded. She got to her feet and looked at Billy. "You know, if this is just a grocery run, I don't see the need to bother *Doctor* Dakota," she said.

"Out of the question, you will have an escort. Your safety is top priority. Besides, two sets of eyes are better than one."

"I don't need to remind you how we met. Besides

keeping you safe, I can also take care of your injuries if need be." Billy's tone mirrored the authority she remembered.

"What if someone gets hurt here?" Kelly said snidely.

"I have an assistant and there are plenty of Magi to hold down the fort until we return."

"He is going, end of discussion," Jonas barked.

"Where are we headed?" Billy asked.

"A small town in the south of Ireland, Nenagh. There is a forest near there. I have circled it on this map. That is supposedly where the first conduit was created. And therefore, where the key would most likely be. Once you find it, get back here immediately," he said, handing her an old, folded map.

"Ireland it is," Billy said.

THE LATE MORNING sun peeked through the scattered clouds as the small Vauxhall Astra barreled down the quiet, winding highway. The tension between Kelly and Billy filled the small cabin of the car.

"It's going to be a long drive if we don't talk," Billy stated casually, checking the rearview mirror.

"The flight was just fine, and we didn't talk then."

"Why are you mad at me?" he snapped, fed up with the tension.

"You know why," she mumbled, staring at the lush rolling landscape, letting it unearth the buried memories.

"Just for argument's sake, let's say I don't."

"You lied, not just once or twice, all the time. I knew there were certain things you claimed to be rez business and couldn't tell me. But it reached the point where you lied more than you told me the truth. You were the first, Will, the first one I ever loved."

"We were kids." He sighed sadly.

"We were eighteen! I gave you everything I had to give —love and trust. It was all destroyed when I caught you coming out of the woods half naked, redressing yourself with..."

"Ember. I told you nothing happened."

"That was a lie, and you know it," she snapped, emotion catching in her throat just as it did all those years ago. Forcing them back into an uncomfortable silence.

"Ember is like me, a shifter," Billy explained fragilely.

"What?" she blurted, part confused, part surprised.

"When we were together, you were like any other human. I had to keep my world a secret. But now," he sighed. "I can tell you everything. In my tribe, when a child turns fourteen, they must complete a rite of passage into adulthood. You might know it as a vision quest. At first everything went as expected, then something happened, something unusual. When I returned and told the village shaman of my visions, I was cast out." Billy fell silent for a moment.

"Skin-walkers are thought of as unnatural creatures and were treated as abhorrent and wretched. I lived on my own for years, never staying in one place for too long. I stumbled upon a group of druids that had stayed hidden over the years. They welcomed me as one of their own and taught me ways to control and use my powers. I stayed with them and watched the world transform from hate and fear into one of understanding. After learning all I could, I ventured out again in search of more like me. Eventually, I ended up close to my home village and ran into someone I knew from childhood who said their child was like me. The elders wouldn't accept me until I proved I wasn't the evil creature they assumed I would become. After demonstrating my abilities to heal and help others, they allowed me back on the reservation and even sent more people to seek my guidance."

Kelly sat listening as she saw him in a new light. He continued, "Shortly after we ended our last tour and I was getting ready to transfer, the council contacted me and offered me a job where I would be able to do the same work I had on the reservation."

"Wait, so how old are you?" Kelly asked.

"Very," he said.

Silence fell once again in the car as Billy pulled into a dirt parking lot near a large group of trees. Billy keyed off the engine and climbed out of the car. Kelly looked around before spotting a small sign next to a gap in the trees.

"Is this it?" she asked.

"According to the GPS," Billy replied. "What are we looking for?"

"A key."

"Obviously, but I doubt it's going to be nailed to a tree with a sign saying, 'magic key.' Was there anything else?" he asked.

"It might be one of those 'you'll know it when you see it' things." Kelly shrugged, starting off onto the narrow trail. Billy a step behind. The farther they went away from the car, the more the modern world slipped away, replaced by the ancient wilderness. A strange feeling pulled at her like an invisible rope tied to her heart. She followed the trail for what seemed like an hour before coming to a sudden stop.

"What is it?" Billy asked.

"I don't know, I just felt like..." she said absentmindedly, her attention being pulled into the thick greenery next to the trail. She stepped through the knee-high ferns; it was like stepping into another world long since forgotten by the hands of time. They weaved their way into the thick green overgrowth. The toe of Kelly's boot caught on a protruding rock, causing her to stumble. Her hand jetted out just in time to catch herself on a stone wall.

"Kelly, are you alright?"

"Yeah, I am fine," she said, examining the wall. It stretched above her several feet, at the top, trace remnants of a thatched roof long since destroyed. She ran her hand along the length, finding a cornerstone, and rounded the corner. A door-like opening parted the wall. A strange sensation came over her, a sense of familiarity. She stepped through the would-be door.

A rush of images flooded her mind. The missing stones from the crumbling walls left from the past completing the walls, the roof appearing out of nothingness and falling into place. Images swirled around her like smoke. The warm glow of a fire grabbed her attention. A woman stoked the small fire under the large iron pot. Her long black hair pulled into a loose braid hidden beneath a piece of cloth. She straightened and turned. Billy crossed between Kelly and the woman by the fire. As he did, the image vanished, dissolving into the air like smoke wafted by a fan. Kelly stared at the large pile of stone in the soot-covered hearth. Other than the chimney caving in, the centuries of unforgiving weather had left it remarkably intact.

"I guess we just start looking around," Billy said. Kelly ignored him, still fixated on the hearth. She moved the pile of stones. Each stone felt like turning a page in the journal, the possibility of finding an answer to a question she hadn't fully formed. *Maybe it's under the next one.*

"I doubt it would be under all that. It's probably buried outside," Billy said, going back out of the ruined home. Kelly continued to unearth the hearth and beneath. Time slipped away with every stone. Her mind played back to the fight with Theo. The fact she had yelled at him, she never stopped to listen to his side of the story because she was so hardheaded. Where was he? She needed to apologize for acting that way. *Maybe if I just listened to his side, it would make more sense.* Pausing, she slumped back on her heels and listened to the footfalls of Billy searching outside. *While you're at it, apologize to Billy. He deserves it.*

Her hands grew numb from the coarse surface of the stones. Each one becoming more painful than the last. Her muscles ached and only half the pile was moved. She couldn't quit. She had to get to the bottom. There was something there. She could feel it in her bones. She grabbed at the next stone. A sharp pain shot through her stomach, causing the stone to slip, tearing at her already raw hands.

"Fuck!" she shouted.

"Are you alright?" a concerned Billy shouted as he flew in the doorway.

"These fucking, god damn..." Kelly growled, hunching over, clutching at her stomach. She took several deep breaths.

"Kelly, just stop for a minute."

"No, I need to finish this. I need to get home." Tears formed in the corners of her eyes.

"Hey, hey, hey. Stop for a minute, talk to me. What's going on?" Billy said, placing a hand on her shoulder.

"I'm in pain... all the time," Kelly gasped, wincing. She dropped her head, trying to push the pain away, ignoring it. A searing white-hot pain slashed across her back. She let out a whimper and sucked air through her teeth. The tight compression on her arms returned with a vengeance as she reached for the stone again; her arms were weak, refusing to hold her weight. Billy caught her as she tumbled to her side. "What is happening?" she said in a whimper.

"I don't know, but we will figure it out. Just relax for a minute. Where does it hurt?" Billy said, propping her up against the small pile she had created.

"My stomach, my back, everywhere," she said, pushing up her sleeves. The faint yellow coils had turned dark purple, the outline more obvious than before. *Chains.*

"Did this happen during training?"

"No, my only injury was with you earlier."

"Okay, I need to take a look at your stomach. Is that okay?" he asked. She nodded. He lifted a corner of her shirt, revealing deeper purple bruises.

"No, that can't be possible, not again. It doesn't make sense," Kelly pleaded.

"You said you're back as well?"

Kelly leaned forward as Billy carefully pulled her shirt up and gingerly touched the matching bruise on her back.

"In the center of each bruise is an almost black line. What do you mean, not again?" he asked.

"I don't know how or what even happened, but last month I was having vivid dreams and I would wake up with bruises. Somehow it was connected to Alexander, and it stopped after I killed him. What is going on?"

"It looks like you were stabbed, but there is no wound, only the bruise. Wait, there is something else." He lifted her shirt higher.

"What is it?"

"More bruises, but they look more like you were beaten with a baseball bat or something," he explained, helping her lean back on the pile.

"Wait here. I will be right back." He darted out of the door. He returned a few minutes later with a small green vial. "Here, I got it from Jonas before we left. Drink this and relax."

"I can't relax. Something's wrong. I need to get back," she said, downing the potion in a single swig.

"And we will. We just need to find the key first, then we will leave," he said.

"I only have a few more stones to move. I know it's somewhere around here, I can feel it," Kelly said, trying to get back to the pile. Even the slightest twitch sent pain shooting through her.

"I will handle these last few stones. Just quit moving," he said. Kelly watched as he removed the final few stones. "Alright, now what?" he said, sitting back on his heels. Kelly got to her knees and crawled over to the hearth, her body still sore, but the pain slowly subsided. She ran her fingers across the base, where she had seen the fire and the iron pot. She pressed and tried to wiggle each stone, but none budged. Her hands worked their way up the back, becoming blacker from the soot and years of dirt.

"Careful, you don't want the whole thing to cave in on you," Billy cautioned. She sat back on her heels in a huff. "What's wrong?"

"It's always in the back wall of the fireplace in the movies," Kelly muttered.

"That's what you're going off of?" he commented dryly.

"No, well, not entirely. I can feel a presence over here but it's so broad I can't pinpoint it," she said, staring blankly at the hearth. The image of the woman blurry reconstructed in her mind. She clenched her eyes, focusing on it, hoping it would come into focus. She closed her hand as if she were holding the rod the woman had used to stoke the fire. The image of the woman cleared only enough for her to see her hands. One held the poker while the other was placed on the side wall of the hearth. Kelly's eyes shot open. She scooted into the hearth, sitting directly where the iron pot would have been.

"Which way is north?" she asked. A confused expression crossed Billy's face as he pointed to the right. Kelly started near the bottom, her hands furiously searching for any loose stones. As her hands worked their way up the wall, her heart hammered in her chest. *It's gotta be here.* Reaching the top of the hearth, she dropped her hands into her lap and leaned against the wall in defeat.

"What's wrong?"

"It's not here."

"Are you sure?" he asked. Kelly dropped her head back against the wall. Her eyes falling on the blackened wall before her. A light breeze tickled the forest canopy, letting a thin ray of light hit the wall. She stared at the small area that it lit.

"The grout is different," she said absentmindedly as she shifted to her knees. She traced the grout with her fingers, cleaning it and outlining a small hand-sized stone. "Hand me a stone, something small with a point, or jagged edge."

A moment later, he handed her a broken shard from another stone. She took the smallest edge and began to scrape and trace the grout along the stone. After a few minutes of grinding away the grout, the stone loosened. She jammed the shard into the gap on one side of the stone and pried it. The stone tumbled out of its home and to the ground. She looked into the hole that remained. There was a small wad of tattered beige cloth pressed flat from the years under the stone. She removed the weighted cloth. Carefully, she scooted out of the fireplace and sat next to

Billy in front of the pile of stones. Gingerly, she unwrapped the weighted object inside. The dull silver medallion was the size of Kelly's palm. Turning it over, the beautiful intricate symbol shone in the light.

"Why does that look familiar?" Billy asked.

"It's the tree of life. See how the roots and branches are all connected," she said.

"So, this is it? This is the key."

"It has to be. Let's go."

CHAPTER
TWENTY-FOUR

The sun had long since set when Kelly and Billy touched back down in Paris, covered in dirt and soot from head to toe. They climbed into the back of the Bentley the council had waiting for them, heading quietly back to Versailles. Kelly's mind was a numbing hum from exhaustion. *Theo should be back by now*. She pulled the sides of her leather jacket tighter, wrapping her arms around her chest. The silver medallion in her pocket squished between her arm and chest. Other than going through security at the airport, she had not let it out of her reach. She had raised suspicions when she first refused to remove her jacket, but then decided it would be fine for the thirty seconds it took to go through the scanner.

She rested her head back, thinking about the million ways her conversation with Theo would go before they all melted away, and the only image that remained was his arms around her and his lip on hers. She couldn't help but smirk. *I miss him, go figure*. It had been a long time since she had felt this way about anyone. Sure, she missed Eric, and her parents, her dog Thor, but that was different. She glanced over at Billy, his head leaning back, and eyes closed. *I have a lot of apologizing to do.* She turned back to the window and watched the blur of lights pass by.

They climbed out of the Bentley onto the deserted sidewalk and headed for the council entrance.

"Hey, er, before we go down, I want to apologize."

"For what?" he asked with a sleepy confusion in his voice.

"Hating you for something you didn't do. I should have believed you all those years ago. I'm sorry."

"You, of all people, should have seen how loyal I am. I always will be."

"Dogs are loyal not cats," Kelly joked; Billy purred jokingly. "Can you forgive me?"

"Of course," he said, closing the metal elevator grate. The cables whined and groaned as the elevator car descended. After a few minutes, they stepped into the council's empty atrium.

"How are you feeling?"

"Still sore as hell. I wonder if Jonas has figured out that shifting potion thing."

Hurried footsteps echoed throughout the atrium.

"Willam, come quick," Autumn shouted, skidding to a stop. They all tore off across the atrium, Kelly pushed down every thought that pulled its way into focus. *Not one of them, please, not one of them.* The faces of Fiona, Omari, Eli, and Theo all taking turns flicking through her mind. *Please no, not them.* Autumn turned sharply down a connecting hall. Slamming a door open, she hurried down a stairwell. Billy leapt from the landing down the stairs to the other. Kelly followed, dropping to her knees at the bottom. They barreled through another door that opened into a large parking garage. Omari was lying on the cement floor. He looked as though he had been thrown down several flights of stairs. He was covered in gouges and bruises. The woman holding his head was just as beat up as he was. Her cropped hair was wild and matted with the blood running down her head. Her fair skin was barely distinguishable between the dirt and blood. A bandage-like cloth was wrapped around her chest and hips like makeshift clothing. Kelly stared in shock at the scene that lay before her.

"Kelly!" Billy shouted, snapping her out of the disconnect she was in.

"Over there in the yellow cabinet there is a med pack and a backboard. I need them both. Go, now!" he commanded. Kelly nodded, darting over to the cabinet. She turned the handle, but it didn't move. She tried again, nothing. It was locked. She took a step back and slammed her foot into the handle several times before it broke off. Grabbing the pack and the board, she sprinted back. Instinctively tossing the bag within arm's reach of Billy and Autumn.

"Let's get him on the board and to the clinic," Billy said. Kelly knelt next to Billy and handed the backboard to Autumn.

"We are going to roll him to us, then you need to slide the board as far under as you can. Okay?" Kelly said, looking at Autumn. Her expression sent an unsettling ripple through Kelly's body. Autumn was always strong, always fearless, but now she was just as scared and in shock as any regular person.

"Autumn, look at me. He's going to be fine. Will is the best." Kelly's eyes connected with hers. "Ready?" she asked. Autumn nodded in confirmation.

"One, two, three," Billy counted. They rolled Omari onto his side. Autumn tucked the board under him and laid him down. Two men in suits came running up to them. It was the driver that picked them up at the airport. Billy strapped Omari to the board, then instructed one man to grab the board and the other to help the woman that had come with him. Autumn and Kelly were left standing alone in the parking garage.

"Are you okay?" Kelly asked, adapting a softer tone to her voice.

"Yes, I-I always lose myself when Omari or Fiona get hurt even after all these years," Autumn said weakly.

"He's going to be okay. Give me a minute to get the mess cleaned up and we will follow them. Do you know what happened?"

"Yes... he..." Autumn struggled to find the words. Kelly stopped picking up the discarded gauze packages and anti-septic wipes.

"What is it?" Kelly asked.

"He went with Theo to the Black Forest."

Kelly's heart slammed into her stomach, knocking the air from her lungs. The packages slipped from her fingers.

"Where... where is—" Kelly asked. Autumn shook her head.

"I don't know. Omari was unconscious when I arrived." Autumn's voice cracked, no longer able to fight back a wave of emotion. Kelly turned on her heel, darting for the door and back up the stairs. The atrium was empty. The door clacked closed behind her as Autumn passed her. Leading her down a hall she had never seen before. They approached a set of double doors with large windows. Omari was on a table being examined by Billy. The woman that had been with him was gone. Autumn's gaze became locked on Omari. Kelly looked around. There was a small waiting room to the right of them and the woman that had been with Omari sat wrapped in a hospital gown and blanket. Kelly stepped into the room.

"Are you okay?" Kelly asked.

"I'm fine. Nothing a little whiskey won't fix," she joked.

"What about your injuries?"

"They'll most likely heal up by morning. I'm Nova," she said, jetting out a hand.

"Kelly," she replied, shaking it. "What happened?"

Nova's voice trembled as she spoke. "There was a trap. Theo and Omari came to talk to my clan about a message the council had received, but we knew nothing about it. When they were leaving, there was an ambush. Another pack of werewolves was waiting for them. They knew Theo and Omari were allies of the council and about Theo's betrayal to Alexander, breaking his hold over him, staying hidden. They wanted to see Alexander succeed. They wanted the world to return to the way it was before—a world of blood and darkness." Kelly's heart dropped as Nova continued. "The Clan heard the howls and the fighting and went to help. We were outmatched. Their numbers alone. It was a massacre. Theo saw it coming and told me to get Omari back here alive and tell the council everything. I didn't want to leave him behind, but I had no choice. It was escape or die." Nova pulled the blanket tighter around her.

"A-And Theo?" Kelly asked, struggling to remain calm as the large knot in her throat impeded her words.

Nova shrugged helplessly, her gaze now fixated on the floor by Kelly's feet. "I wish I could tell you he was okay, but I have no clue."

I don't think he is. Kelly left the waiting room and headed for the atrium. Hilda and her guards exited the courtroom Fiona's trial had been held in.

"Counselor, can I speak with you?" Kelly shouted, jogging up to her.

"I have a moment. How can I help you?" Hilda said, scribbling on a document one of her guards held.

"Did you know about Theo's mission to the Black Forest?" Kelly asked.

"I was briefed on the matter. The Evercrest Clan refuses to maintain a headquarters here, so we must send envoys out every so often to meet with them, hear their concerns and such." Hilda's clinically detached answer dug at Kelly.

"There was an ambush waiting for Theo and Omari. The Clan has been massacred, Omari and a woman named Nova—" Kelly broke off in a shriek of pain, dropping to the floor. A blast of white-hot pain formed a line across her chest. Another explosion radiated through her back. Cold tile pressed against her cheek, then darkness.

A BLINDING bright light woke Kelly, a wave of panic raced through her. Glancing around, she realized she was now in one of the medical exam rooms. Hilda sat next to the exam table Kelly was on, her bodyguards outside the door. Kelly's leather jacket draped across the chair.

"I have sent for Jonas. He should be here soon."

"What happened?" Kelly asked, wincing at the pain now radiating through her body.

"You screamed, then collapsed at my feet," Hilda explained. "Tell me, what happened right before you passed out?"

"There was this pain. Like fire tearing at my skin. Only a thousand times worse," Kelly described.

"Where?"

"My chest, my back." Kelly motioned, only to be greeted with a dull throb.

"Do you mind showing me?" Hilda asked, getting to her feet.

Kelly hesitated for a moment, then pulled at the collar of her shirt, revealing the edge of a long, dark pink burn. As she glanced at it, she thought back to the other phantom injuries. She lifted the corner of her shirt, revealing the bruises from before. They had faded to a rough brownish yellow.

"What the fuck?" she mumbled, shifting her position, then flinching in pain.

"As I thought," Hilda said, then turned to her bodyguards and spoke in a sharp language Kelly didn't know. Her bodyguard nodded and left, then she returned to Kelly's side.

"What do you know about that symbol on your arm?"

"Absolutely nothing, it just appeared."

"When?"

"A few weeks ago. Theo drank some of my blood so that he would be strong enough to escape Alexander's mansion," Kelly answered. A smile crossed Hilda's lips.

"What else?"

"He has one too, but it's different."

"That is because you are living, and he isn't... technically," Hilda explained. "It is the symbol for soulmates or everlasting love."

"I'm sorry what?" Kelly blurted.

"In most human cases, you can only assume the person you love is who you are meant to be with. Humans fall in and out of so-called love a thousand times over in their lifetime, yet very few actually find their soulmate. In the supernatural world it means much more, it not only means you will be able to find them anywhere, but you also protect each other no matter the cost, you trust them without a single doubt, and you share each other's pain."

"But Theo and I-I don't... we just... we aren't." Kelly sputtered over her words.

"How long have you felt these pains?"

"A couple days now, ever since..." Kelly paused.

"Ever since he went to the Black Forest?" Hilda finished. Kelly nodded. Her bodyguard returned and handed her a small green vial.

"Drink this. It will numb any residual pain you have for a while. Omari is awake, and Autumn is with him." Kelly swigged back the potion and felt the relief run through her.

"What about Fiona?"

"She will be escorted to them shortly." Hilda headed for the door.

"Is there anything I can do to get her sentence forgiven or changed?" Kelly asked.

"I'm afraid not. She must face the consequences of her actions like anyone else," Hilda said sadly. Once Hilda and her guards were out of sight, Kelly grabbed her jacket off the chair and felt for the pocket the medallion was in. She breathed a sigh of relief and slipped her jacket on.

She hesitated outside Omari's room. Autumn was on one side of his bed, holding his hand and Fiona on the other. One happy family reunited. Her eyes fell on Autumn and Omari and the way they looked at each other. *That's what soulmates look like.* A knot formed in her chest as she lightly knocked on the door.

"Kelly, come in, come in." Omari smiled.

"How are you feeling?"

"Oh, I will be fine. I have my wonderful girls." He gazed

lovingly at each of them, then turned his attention back to her.

"I just wanted to stop in and say hi. I need to go speak with Jonas and see if he knows what to do."

"Theo is strong." His elation was replaced with actuality.

"Even his strength has limits," Kelly said.

CHAPTER
TWENTY-FIVE

Kelly burst through the front door of Jonas's house; a strange calmness hung in the air as if the house was empty. She hurtled up the stairs two at a time to find Jonas still in the chair he had been in before she left for Ireland.

"Jonas," she said, stepping into the room. "Are you awake? Jonas?"

He groggily opened his eyes with a sigh, only to be cut short by a wretched, hacking cough. His body shuddered as he hunched forward, and Kelly leapt to his side, handing him the cup of water left there.

"Take a sip slowly."

"I'm fine, did you find it?" he croaked.

"Yes, we found it. Have you been in this chair all day?"

"I just... got so tired." Removing his glasses, he rubbed the tiredness from his eyes.

"Come on, let's get you to bed. You'll be more comfortable there." Kelly held out her hand to him.

"No, I want to see the key," he said with determination.

"I'll show it to you once you are in bed." Kelly's authoritative tone was similar to his own. He weakly pulled the blanket off his lap and gripped the arms of his chair, struggling to lift himself up. Kelly bent, pulling his arm over her shoulder.

"On three, here we go. One, two," she counted, pulling him onto his feet. Wrapping her arm around his waist, she led him down the hall to his room.

It was an otherwise nondescript room, except for a few pieces of furniture: a wispy blanket draped the pristinely made double bed; its companion, a patchwork quilt, folded neatly at the bottom; a plain dresser with a vanity mirror hung above it; in one corner sat a high wing-backed chair with a floor lamp tucked behind it; and last, a small end table by the bedside containing a reading lamp, an empty glass, and a book. Kelly carefully lowered him onto the bed, then knelt, removed his house slippers, and tucked him in under the quilt.

"That is better, thank you," he said. Kelly reached into her inside pocket and retrieved the tattered cloth with the medallion inside. She slipped it into his hand. He unfolded the cloth with care. The silver tree of life was large and shimmered in the light, its beauty evident.

"We found the house. It's in ruins now, but the strangest thing happened. When I stepped through the doorway, it was like I saw into the past. There was a woman by a hearth and—" Kelly began, her excitement getting the better of her before Jonas erupted into another fit of coughs. Picking up the empty glass, she ran down the hallway to the bathroom. After handing him the cool glass of water, he took a sip and said nothing, only nodded.

She hurried off down the stairs to his study; clawing through several stacks of books and papers, she found a rotary dial phone from the 1930s. Lifting the receiver, she was greeted by the low drone of the dial tone. *Shit I don't know Will's number.* Suddenly, a woman's voice came from the other end of the line.

"Hello, how may I direct your call, Professor Wainwright?"

"Doctor Dakota, please," Kelly answered.

"One moment," the woman said. The line clicked, then trilled.

"Hello?" a groggy Billy answered.

"Hey, it's Kelly. Can you come over to Jonas's? I think something is wrong."

"Sure thing. I'll be right over."

Kelly placed the receiver on the hook and returned to Jonas's room. He was turning the medallion over in his hands, admiring the craftsmanship and its condition.

"I called Doc. He should be here in a few minutes."

"I don't need a doctor. I am fine."

"Too bad, he's coming over and he's going to take a look at you," Kelly said. Jonas glanced up from the medallion, his normally hard, stoic face softened.

"You have a lot of her in you," he said, a nostalgic smirk pulled at his lip.

"Who?"

"Emily, you have her stubbornness and her rebellious qualities. She would have loved to know you." A lamented silence fell as he turned his attention back to the medallion. "That is why I acted the way I did. I didn't see *you*. I saw Emily, and I tried to protect you like I did her."

"You don't need to protect me; I have always been the one that protects others, and I wouldn't have it any other way."

"I know that now. I see you for you, my great-great-great-granddaughter."

The door opened downstairs, followed by footsteps climbing the stairs. Billy entered the room carrying a small medical bag.

"I'll just be in the next room," Kelly said, closing the bedroom door behind her.

She wandered into the library and sat in Jonas's chair, cradling her head in her hands and closing her eyes. *I need to find Theo, but I can't just leave Jonas in his condition. Whatever that may be.* Kelly got out of her seat and paced around the room. She took in the messy table where a couple of vials were cradled in the spine of an open book alongside an envelope from the council mentioning a finance meeting; the wax seal clung firmly to the side. She paced, her mind racing with all the things that needed to be done. A glimpse of a book on the floor caught her eye—it was Jonas's book, which he had been reading that morning before they left. Without thinking, she picked it up and began flicking through its pages, tracing the jagged symbols with her fingertips. They felt strangely familiar, similar to the symbols on the council's seal, but different. This must have been the Lepontic script Jonas had been laboriously translating. Instead of trying to read it, she admired the beautiful penmanship and artistic effort put into the pages until her eyes settled on a picture of a vase with two sweeping handles extending from the opening at its top down to its broad base and was adorned with a painted picture of warriors fighting.

Billy came into the room. She snapped the book closed and got to her feet.

"What's the verdict?" she asked.

"Well, it's strange," he murmured while running his fingers through his hair.

"What do you mean?"

"In the years that I have known him, Jonas has never had a cold, allergies or any other ailments one would associate with normal human life."

"So, he's got a cold that has just compounded over the past century?" Kelly concluded.

"No, he doesn't display any symptoms that would lead to that."

"Then what?"

Billy simply shrugged. "In short, old age."

"How? When I got here, he was as spry as an average fifty-year-old. You're telling me something just hit the fast-track button on his age-meter."

"What do you know about being a conduit?" he asked.

"A handful of stuff. I'm still learning. I know that when Jonas became one, his grandfather had been dead for about five years, so there was no one to show him the ropes."

The room fell quiet as Kelly fit the pieces into place. She rushed past Billy and into Jonas's bedroom.

"Have there ever been two conduits alive at one time?" she asked.

"Not as far as I'm aware," he replied in a tired voice. "It would usually pass down from one generation to the next. But you are an exception—it bypassed at least two generations, and it didn't remain within the male lineage."

"That must be it!" Kelly exclaimed, turning toward Billy. "I'm weakening him. Maybe if I put some distance between us, he will recover. Will you stay here with him? See if you can find some kind of remedy?"

"Where are you going?" Billy asked.

"To the Black Forest," she said.

TWENTY-SIX

K elly raced down the hall, eyeing the names and titles scrawled on the doors. She stopped in front of one that read "High Chancellor – Council of the Eternals." She pounded on the door. A moment later a towering bodyguard answered with a scowl.

"I need to speak with the chancellor. It's an emergency."

"Humans, always exaggerating," the man groaned.

"What is it, Ms. Frost?" Hilda asked from behind the bodyguard.

"It's Jonas. He's dying!" Kelly exclaimed. "Doctor Dakota is trying to find a way to save him, or at least slow it down. I am going to go to the Black Forest to rescue Theo."

The bodyguard moved aside to let Hilda take his place.

"I won't allow you to proceed with such a dangerous move," she declared. "I understand your worry, but it's far too risky—especially in light of what occurred with the Evercrest clan. We still don't know who attacked and for what reason."

"Theo is being tortured; I don't know how much longer he can hold on."

"I am sorry, but I cannot authorize it."

"I'm not asking for permission. Unlike Jonas, I will not sit idly by and let others run errands for me. I would never let someone be left behind," Kelly said.

"You will do no such thing, return to your quarters. One of my men will be by to escort you to Jonas's."

Kelly stormed the hall. Once she heard the door latch shut behind her, she whipped her head around to make sure no one was following her, then raced toward the clinic.

Pausing outside Omari's room, she peered in to find Autumn and Omari talking in hushed tones, while Fiona lay with her head resting against Omari's bed. They spoke a dialect that was most likely long forgotten. "Sorry to interrupt, but there isn't a lot of time. Omari, how are you feeling?"

He paused, scanning Kelly's expression. "I am ready to get out of this bed."

"Just say the word and we are with you," Autumn said.

"I'm going too," Fiona chimed.

"I appreciate that, but you were just sentenced by the council."

"Theo is like a brother to me. I am going."

"I will talk with Hilda when we return," Autumn stated.

"Fuck. Alright. Can you break whatever chains or bindings hold Fiona here?"

"That shouldn't be a problem."

"Do you have a way of contacting Eli?" Kelly asked. Autumn pulled her phone from her skirt pocket and tossed it to her. She found his number and tapped the call button. The line trilled for a moment before he answered.

"Hey, Autumn, what's up?"

"It's Kelly. Where are you?"

"Paris. Just got off the plane. Should be back in about an hour."

"Wait for us there. Get five tickets to Berlin."

"Why, what's going on?"

"We are going to get Theo back." Kelly hung up the phone and tossed it back to Autumn. "Meet me in the parking garage in five minutes," Kelly said, taking off back down the hall.

Her heart hammered as she burst into her room, retrieving the dagger from under her pillow and strapping it to her leg before hurrying off again through the atrium.

When the elevator reached the lobby, she wrenched the metal gate open and ran for Jonas's house once again, bursting through the door and hurrying into his lab. She rooted through the small vials on the table, stuffing two of the familiar shimmering green potions into her jacket. Partially hidden beneath a piece of paper, a flicker of blue caught her attention; it was the blue potion she had used to shapeshift. She grabbed it and tucked it into her jean pocket as Billy descended the stairs, pausing in the doorway.

"What's going on?" he asked, watching her rummage through Jonas's things.

"I'm going to find out why the Evercrest Clan was ambushed and bring Theo back. Stay here and watch over Jonas."

"Kelly, you don't have to do this. We can find someone else."

"There is no one else. The council won't help. I am all there is!" she snapped, her assertive tone ruder than she intended. Their eyes connecting for the first time. The heavy reality of her not returning was all too familiar, and the emotion in his eyes sent her back to the cool desert night standing outside the mess hall tent. The weight of wartime reality setting in. Her convoy was leaving in a few hours for a nearby village where they were to repair the roadway after a recent mortar attack.

"Be safe, okay," he said meekly, stepping to the side to let her pass.

"Call Autumn if anything changes," she said, her voice raspy and uneasy as she closed the door behind her.

The elevator lurched to a halt and as she stepped out, she heard two voices murmuring in the distance. Making her way toward the entryway into the atrium, she spotted the guards at the same time they noticed her. *Shit.* She burst into a sprint, the sound of her echoing footsteps bouncing off the walls as door after door flew by in a blur.

Crashing through the door to the stairwell leading to the parking garage. Kelly stumbled into the door at the bottom of the stairs, wrenching it open. Getting to her feet, she looked up and saw one of the black Bentleys in front of her idling. The blackened window rolled down. "Get in," Autumn called from the driver's seat. Kelly dove into the passenger seat as the tires screeched into action. Leaving the guards behind.

The Bentley barreled its way down the sparse French highway, Kelly's leg bobbing in anxiety. *Come on, come on.* Kelly glanced over Autumn's shoulder at the speedometer. *One hundred eighty. Hold on, Theo, we are coming.* A surge of pain crossed her jaw. She clutched at it, then another searing pain shot through her shoulder. Kelly let out a grunt of pain. "God damn it," she shouted, pounding her fist into the side of the car.

"Are you okay?" Fiona asked.

"Theo, he's hurt bad. They are torturing him, like it's some kind of game." Kelly groaned.

"How do you know?" Omari asked from the front seat.

"I just do," she snapped, her eyes closed tight trying to maintain composure while enduring the pain. Omari exchanged a concerned look with Autumn.

The sound of the engine filled the silence.

CHAPTER
TWENTY-SEVEN

Autumn expertly weaved the rented Opel Astra off the busy highway and down the slender city roadways before turning onto a deserted back road. Coming to a stop outside an odd-looking cabin. The Bavarian-style exterior forced a childhood memory of her mother's voice reading "Hansel and Gretel." *Finally, they saw the house of cakes and bread.* She climbed out of the car and scanned the surrounding forest for a path or indication of where to begin. Omari ran into the cabin while the others climbed out of the car. A moment later, he returned with a small satchel draped over his shoulder.

"What's that?" Kelly asked him.

"I made a call at the airport for some supplies," he said. Kelly gave him a confused look. "It's blood for Theo. We can't afford for him to feed off you again. We don't know the situation at hand," he said, tightening the strap so it clung to him.

"Is that enough?"

"There is never enough blood when it comes to a hungry vampire," Omari mused.

"What is this place?"

"A safe house of sorts. The Evercrest clan preferred to roam the forest but would use it to store emergency items like clothes, potion ingredients, dry goods," he explained, removing the top from a miniature mason jar then drinking the orange liquid inside.

"You guys go ahead; we are right behind you," Autumn said. Omari wrapped his arms around her and kissed her deeply, then nodded to Kelly.

"Was that a health potion or something?" she asked.

"It is for additional strength and speed; you are much faster now." Omari smiled. "Follow me. I believe I know where they are holding Theo."

They took off across the yard and into the thick forest. Swerving around large trees and boulders. Kelly sprinted, keeping in time with Omari. They cut through a cold shallow river, then came to a stop. Omari tucked behind a large boulder. Kelly did the same. Omari held his finger to his lips, then pointed to the other side of where they were. Kelly carefully leaned far enough to see a handful of people surrounding the mouth of a cave.

"What's the plan?" Kelly asked, returning to her position next to Omari.

"There are two werewolves, two shifters and at least one witch, maybe two. I can probably handle two, maybe three on my own, but we don't know how many may be hiding inside."

"Where are the others?" Kelly whispered, searching the direction they had come.

"There was only enough of the potion for one. Since I knew where to go, Autumn stayed to make more. Don't worry, they should be here in a moment."

Kelly grunted, collapsing to her side as a white-hot pain

shot across her stomach. Omari covered her mouth, trying to stay quiet.

"We don't have time to wait," she whispered between heavy pained breaths.

"Attacking on our own would be suicide."

"Fine. But we aren't going to just sit here and wait to be discovered. Let's even the odds." She scanned their surroundings, then peeked out from behind the boulder again.

A small fire crackled under a large cast-iron pot on one side of the cave as three men casually stood around it. Kelly recognized one of them as Rachel's date from Delirium. The muted snap of a branch sent her bolting back, pressing her body into the bolder. They held their breath, listening to the sentry's footsteps coming closer, then stopped. *Turn around, turn around.* Omari grabbed a small rock and crept in front of her. He threw it farther into the forest. The sentry walked past them to investigate the sound. Omari sprang up, wrapping his arm around the sentry's neck. The sentry writhed and squirmed, trying to break free. Struggling to maintain control, Omari tightened his hold. The sentry's squirming lessened until he went limp. Omari repositioned himself, then lowered the sentry behind a nearby fallen tree. He returned to his place next to her.

"One down," he whispered.

"A hundred to go," Kelly finished as she peered around the boulder.

"Oi, Sergei, soups on," Rachel's date called from the fireside.

"Nah, mate, he's German int he?"

"Ugh, well then, what's German for 'come get some bloody food?'"

"Roden," the third man answered. Poking the base of

the fire, a flicker of light illuminated his face. His black hair, tawny skin and the four distinct pink scars across his face. *He was at Alexander's.*

"Sergei, Rodent! Is he deaf or something?"

"Instead of shouting for the entire forest to hear, how about you walk your lazy ass over there and get him," the third man snarled at the first.

"Alright, alright, no need to get your knickers in a twist," the first man said as he headed toward Kelly and Omari's boulder.

Kelly glanced at Omari, who was already in position to attack the way he had before. He jerked his head toward the small footpath on the other side of the boulder. She snaked her way over to it. The trail wrapped around the makeshift campsite. *Must be from the patrols.* She glanced back at Omari, who gave her a confirming nod just as the man stepped past the boulder and spotted them.

"Hey!" he shouted. Omari leapt up, covering his mouth, hurtling them both to the ground, followed by a muffled crunch, and the man went limp. She took off in a crouched run down the trail, stopping behind a large tree. Kelly touched the dagger on her thigh as she peered out. The remaining guards, now on their feet, were only a short distance away.

"Something's not right," the man from Alexander's said, exchanging a look with another guard. Kelly felt a poke, then pressure in her head. She took a steadying breath and focused, remembering her training with Evalyn.

"Probably just a bear." The guard shrugged.

The man from Alexander's glared at him before he shifted fluidly into his massive wolf form. He sniffed at the air then jerked his head, indicating for them to split up. She waited till the wolf was alone. Slipping out from behind the tree, it lunged for her, a large blur of fur slamming into her with such force that they skidded along the forest floor. His sharp teeth dug into her shoulder. A painful shriek erupted from her. She pounded her fist against his head as his teeth sank deeper. Ripping the pendant from her neck, she plunged the point into its neck just below his jaw. With a desperate yelp, the wolf stumbled backward, pawing at the part still protruding from its neck, giving her a chance to pull the dagger from its sheath. With reckless determination, she tackled it, thrusting the blade into its side until it pierced its heart, covering her in hot mahogany blood. She removed it, getting to her feet in time to see Omari and the others taking out the remaining guards. Kelly looked at each of them, then nodded at Omari and turned into the mouth of the cave.

THE CAVERN EXPANDED into a large room before her, pillars of earth supporting the momentous ceiling. A set of natural stone steps descended into the earth. Kelly peered, catching a flicker of light stretching up from the cavern floor. There was a large fire burning in the center of the room and several people scattered around it. Chained to a large rock wall was Theo, his clothes torn to shreds, exposing his injuries. Kelly placed a hand on her own stomach as her eyes fell to the large slice on Theo's. Kelly snarled. Every fiber of her body wanted to rip each of them limb from limb. A hand tugged at the collar of her jacket. Autumn helped ease it off and examined her bloodied shoulder.

"Are you alright?" she asked.

"Yeah, I'll be fine."

"One shifter, two werewolves, three Magi," Autumn

whispered. "There is a fae here somewhere, but I'm unsure where."

"Fiona, Autumn and I, take the magi. Kelly, you take the shifter and get to Theo," Eli directed.

"And I will take the rest," Omari smiled.

"The second someone is available, get to Theo," Eli added. They nodded in agreement. Kelly stared slack-jawed at Eli.

"What? You're not the only one that's been training."

Kelly turned back to look at the scene below, planning the best method of attack.

"Let me get close enough to throw this, then head for the shifter. He's the closest to Theo," Eli said, holding up a glass vial filled with a black liquid. Popping the cork off, he pulled a hair from his head and placed it in the liquid. He then looked at the others, who all did the same. Once everyone had added their hair, he held it up to Kelly. She furrowed her brow.

"It's magic smoke, I guess. By adding our essence, once I throw it, we will be the only ones who can see through it. But it only lasts for a minute, so we have to be fast," Eli instructed. She pulled a hair and added it to the vial. He shook it vigorously.

"Ready?" he asked. They nodded, creeping close behind him as they made their way to the cavern floor.

Just out of range of the firelight, Eli tossed the vial next to the fire, shattering upon impact. A cloud of pitch-black smoke engulfed the area. Kelly and the others watched as the guards got to their feet and pawed at the darkness. The smoke for Kelly was like water, rippling and distorting images. The guards' confusion masked the sound of their footsteps as they slipped past. Kelly removed her knife from its sheath as quickly as she could, snuck up behind the shifter, covered his mouth with one hand, and dragged the blade across his throat with the other. With a muffled sputtering, he fell to the ground into a pool of its own blood.

Kelly turned. The path to Theo was now clear. His head was tilted back, resting on the rock behind him. His eyes flitted open. A look of panic flicked across his face for a fraction of a second, then savage. His solid black eyes landed on hers. A sudden pressure pushed at her mind. She whirled around, searching for the source. Fiona swirled her arms, magically knocking her opponent to the ground. Eli was locked in an intense exchange of blows with his opponent when Autumn landed a final blow to hers, then headed for Eli. As the pressure grew, she collapsed, clutching at her head, digging her nails into her scalp.

Writhing on the cavern floor, she struggled to apply her training. The only tangible thoughts being the indescribable pain and failure. She had failed to rescue Theo. Opening her eyes, she spotted a man standing in the entrance to a tunnel, deep purple smoke emanating from his skin, a sinister smile rooted on his face. A voice not her own stabbed at her mind. *Weak. Pathetic. Failure. You will never be strong enough. You have failed and now you and all you love will die.* She truly believed her mind was about to burst when the pressure vanished. Kelly looked over to see Autumn yanking out a knife from the man's chest. Pulling herself off the ground, Kelly got back on her feet.

"Behind you!" Eli shouted. A heavy force tackled Kelly from the side, launching her into a nearby rock. Knocking her head and the air from her lungs. Rolling on the ground, she gulped the air until her breath returned to normal before getting to her hands and knees. She looked up at the remaining werewolf. Roughly twice the size of an Alaskan timber wolf.

She pulled the small blue vial from her pocket, drained the contents. Gritting her teeth as the familiar fire burned under her skin, her bones cracking and reforming. She stifled the urge to scream as her body stretched and twisted into its monstrous form.

Kelly snarled and snapped her teeth at it. It let out a nasty, bone-chilling growl. She steadied her stance. Out of the corner of her eye, she caught a flicker of movement. Eli and the others were working their way over to them. *I need to distract him so they can get Theo free.* Kelly pushed off hard on the ground, tackling the wolf. It wriggled beneath her and snapped its jaws, whipping its head around as it wriggled. Kelly lost her balance. Taking advantage, the wolf clamped its mouth around her forearm, thrashing it around. Kelly felt her flesh tear and her bones break under its immense pressure. She let out a howl, swatting at its head. The wolf hung on, refusing to let go. Kelly took a breath, then dug her long-clawed thumb into its eye until the wolf went limp. A stomach-churning squelch sounded as she removed her claw from its skull and let the body fall next to her. She rolled onto all fours and watched as her smoky gray claws shifted back to her natural pale hands covered in blood and the few clumps of pink, gray tissue beneath her nails. She vomited, unsure whether it was from disgust or shock at her actions. The image of her thumb deep in the wolf's skull seared itself into her mind.

That was its brain. I dug my nail into its brain. Tears burned in her eyes. The metallic clink of chain on stone accompanied by vicious grunts pulled her attention to Theo still chained to the boulder. She got to her feet, wiping away the tears and bile from her face, then headed for him. His eyes were strange. The large black orbs were gray and filmy. Kelly exchanged a concerned look with Eli. Then shifted back to Theo's ravenous expression. He pulled against the chains, unfazed as they burned his flesh. With every jerk, bits of stone fell to the ground.

"He's been drugged. Look around and see if you can find any clues as to what it might be," Autumn said, standing next to Kelly. They began searching through a pile of bags and boxes sitting by the fire.

"I found a bottle, it says Eph... Eph..." Eli struggled.

"*Ephedra sinica*," Omari corrected. "And Belladonna." He held up another small bottle.

"Devil's tears," Fiona gasped.

"What does that mean? Is he going to be okay? Can you cure him?" Kelly asked. A crack rang through the cavern. All attention turned to Theo, one of his arms now free from the boulder.

"The poison in his system stops his ability to tell friends from foe or food, for that matter. I should be able to make an antidote, but I need time. Can you keep him busy?" Autumn said, pulling vials and herbs out of a satchel.

"Not like I have a choice." Kelly shrugged as another crack filled the air. Theo was free. He lurched forward, Omari in his sights. Kelly tackled him. He writhed under her. Jabbing his elbow into her ribs. She clutched at it as she fell to her side. He got to his feet and landed a kick to her stomach. *I can't just be a punching bag; I need to fight back. But I don't want to hurt him. He's drugged. He won't stop.*

He went to kick her again. She grabbed his leg as it impacted and rolled, hurtling him to the hard ground. He rolled onto his back and rammed his heel into her face. A soft crunch echoed in her head as blood poured from her nose. She clutched her face, tears welling from the pain and the gnawing reminder.

It is *Theo. This is what he's capable of.* Focus. *Save your friends.*

Theo got to his feet while Kelly struggled to hers, wiping the blood from her face. Fiery knuckles cracked against her jaw, sending her to one knee.

"Just a little longer," Autumn called.

Kelly let out every ounce of frustration and twisted, confused emotion she had bottled up in one core-shaking scream. She pushed off the ground, hurtling herself toward the deranged rabid vampire that put her insides in knots. He jabbed his fist toward her. Kelly's hand shot up, grabbing his wrist and jabbing him in the side. Theo stumbled, hunched over in pain.

"It's ready. We need to get him to drink this."

Kelly's attention flicked to Autumn. Theo rushed forward, slamming Kelly into the boulder he had been shackled to. Her knees buckled, sending her crashing to the ground. He placed his hands on the rock above her, ready to drive his foot into her again. She rammed her foot into his crotch. He collapsed onto the ground. Fighting back overwhelming exhaustion, Kelly scrambled over to Theo, pushing him onto his back, pinning him to the ground. He snarled, craning his head, attempting to bite anything in his way. Kelly let out a pained groan as she struggled against his writhing body. Omari swooped around, taking control of Theo's head. Fiona and Eli anchored his legs. Autumn dug her fingers into his cheeks, squeezing his mouth open, poured the antidote into his mouth, then forced it closed.

He writhed and strained against the group before falling limp. Hesitantly, each let go, first Autumn, Omari, then Fiona, followed by Eli. Kelly, still sprawled across Theo's chest, didn't move.

"It's okay, you can let go." Autumn placed a gentle hand on her shoulder. Kelly shifted herself and collapsed onto him, wrapping her arms around him.

"Please be okay. Please be okay. I'm so sorry," she whispered, burying her face in his neck as she was unable to fight back her tears. *Not this one. God, please. Not this one. I need him.* His ragged, shallow breaths were the only sign of life. Seconds felt like hours as every happy memory she had with him spun through her mind.

"What for?" he said with a slight groan. Kelly shot up.

"You're awake," she breathed, throwing herself back over him. A grunt of pain caused her to spring back up. "Sorry."

He placed a hand on her cheek. "What happened to your face? Did I? Oh, my darling," he groaned, forcing himself into a sitting position. "There are no words for how grieved I am for what I have done."

"It's fine, I'm fine. You were poisoned and weren't yourself. But you're okay now."

"Okay is a bit generous. However, I am alive. Thanks to you." Theo smiled at her.

"Me? I didn't do anything," Kelly said.

"You disobeyed the council," Omari chimed.

"You risked your life to save me." Theo continued, "You have nothing to apologize for. If anyone has to apologize, it is me."

"But the way I left. Not letting you explain." She blubbered. "I could have lost you."

"You could never lose me, my darling." Theo wiped the tears from her cheeks. "You were right. I should have told you about Jonas. For that I apologize."

"Jonas! Shit, we need to get back." Kelly got to her feet.

"What has happened?" Theo asked, taking the blood bag Eli handed to him.

"Jonas is dying. I left him with Billy to find an answer, but they need help. Let's see if these guys have anything on them that might tell us who they are and get out of here," Kelly said.

They spread out, each taking a body. Kelly looked at where she had fought the werewolf. It had shifted back to its human form. The woman lay naked on her side as if sleeping, her head resting in a pool of blood. The memory of the spongy inside of her skull made Kelly's stomach twist into knots. She moved to the next body and patted its pockets but didn't find anything.

"Any luck?" she asked the others. A resounding chorus of "no" responded. They made their way back to the mouth of the cave. The bodies, still where they had left them. Kelly walked over to the pile of belongings next to the now extinguished fire. She tossed a black t-shirt to Theo. He smiled, removed the remains of his tattered shirt, and slipped on the other.

As the others continued to search, Kelly stood over the werewolf from Alexander's mansion. Crouching, she rolled him onto his back when she spotted a tattoo on his forearm.

"*Exsurgat diabolus et infernus in terra*?" Kelly attempted. The others walked over to her.

"Let the devil rise and bring hell on earth," Autumn said. An ominous weight filled the air.

AS THEY REACHED the edge of the forest, the trees thinned, giving way to the darkened Bavarian cabin and the rented

Opel Astra parked out front waiting for them. Kelly glanced around at the group, exhausted, covered in dirt, sweat, and blood. Omari and the others reached for the Astra's doors.

"Hang on a sec. Omari, you said this is a safe house, right? Medical supplies, food, clothes?" Kelly asked.

"That's correct."

"We should get cleaned up enough to get back to the council. If we try to go through airport security like this, we may raise some unwanted questions," Kelly stated.

"There isn't any running water, but there is a well around the back. I will get some water," Omari said, heading for the well while the others headed for the cabin.

"Not alone," Kelly called. Eli took off at a jog, catching up to Omari.

CHAPTER
TWENTY-EIGHT

As Kelly stepped off the plane in Paris, a strange energy stirred up inside her chest. Unsurprisingly, there was no car from the council waiting to pick them up. Autumn secured the last rental car they needed, and they drove off to Versailles.

"Just drop me off near Jonas's place. I've got this weird feeling," Kelly said.

They arrived at an ominous cloud of smoke coming from the direction of Jonas's house. Kelly stumbled out of the car, running toward his home and watched as black smoke poured out of the windows. Without hesitating, she threw open the door to find Jonas lying on the floor in the hallway leading to his study. Kelly dropped, trying to pick up his unconscious body. Theo dragged her back to the street.

"Stay here. I will get him," Theo said, darting into the house. A moment later he returned cradling an unconscious Jonas in his arms. In the distance, sirens blared, shattering the night's silence. Theo and Kelly exchanged glances, then tore off down the street to the council.

The lobby was empty: the woman behind the desk had gone. They rushed into the elevator, wrenching the gate closed and descending to the atrium.

The elevator shuddered to a stop at the darkened atrium; several of the lights overhead clinked and fizzled. As they stepped farther in, the flickering light illuminated the splattered blood and lifeless bodies. Kelly and Theo exchanged worried glances, then headed for Billy's clinic. Eerie silence filled the hall. Kelly opened the blood-splattered door to the small examination room. Thankfully, it remained untouched; they hurried inside. Theo placed Jonas on the examination table. Jonas stirred, coughing, and wheezing as he regained consciousness.

Kelly rummaged through the cabinets before finding a small stack of plastic cups. She took one of them, filled it with water, then she handed the cup to Jonas. Theo helped prop him up as Jonas sipped.

"What happened?" she asked.

"Doctor Dakota got a call. Something about the clinic. So, he left. Said he'd only be gone a few minutes, but that was some time ago," Jonas said hoarsely.

"How did your house catch on fire?" Kelly asked. Jonas looked up at her in confusion.

"I needed to look something up and he hadn't returned, so I went to get it myself. I got lightheaded. I must have bumped into the table and knocked something over. When I saw how quickly the fire was spreading, I went to call emergency services. The smoke must have gotten to me," he explained with a level of confusion that worried Kelly.

"We need to find Will. Maybe he knows what happened," Kelly said.

"We should also have the others meet us here," Theo said.

"Do you mind staying here and watching over him? I promise I will shout if I need help. I'll be back in a few minutes," Kelly asked. Theo nodded. She cracked the door and watched the empty hall for a moment, then slipped out. Just before the door clicked shut, she heard Jonas's rough, weary voice. "Emily may have been your wife, but she's the one that makes you complete."

Pretending she hadn't heard the private moment, she clicked the door closed. She cautiously crossed the atrium and slipped through the door down to the parking garage. The stairwell was empty and untouched. Reaching the bottom of the stairs, she opened the door enough to see out. Spotting the others, she relaxed a little and swung the door open.

"Kelly, what happened? Is everything okay?" Autumn asked.

"No. Jonas's house caught fire, and the Council has been attacked."

"What do you mean, attacked?" Omari asked.

"I haven't found any survivors. Theo and I took Jonas to Will's clinic. Let's head over there and figure out what to do. Prepare yourself," she cautioned, pulling the door to the stairwell open.

Kelly and the others had almost crossed the atrium when they heard a sound coming from across the room. She gestured for them to keep walking while Omari hesitated. Kelly glanced at him reassuringly, and he raised three fingers in response. Kelly nodded. Removing her dagger from its sheath, she headed off toward the noise. Spotting a large trail of blood smeared across the floor; something had clearly been dragged through it. At the end of the trail was a door labeled "SUPPLIES." Kelly cautiously gripped the bloodied handle and prepared herself for anything that might happen, then pushed it open. Inside were shelves of paper products and cleaning items, along with Hilda propped up against the wall between the sink and an empty mop bucket. Kelly grabbed some paper towels and hurried over.

"What happened?"

"There were so many, we didn't have a chance," Hilda gasped, clutching at the wound on her stomach. Kelly carefully pulled Hilda's hands away. Blood gushed like water. She wadded a bunch of paper towels and pressed it hard against her stomach.

"Keep pressure," Kelly said, searching around for something to hold it in place. "How long ago did this happen?"

"I'm not sure, could have been a few minutes, an hour, maybe more," Hilda said through gasps of pain.

"I need to get Autumn. She can help," Kelly said, getting to her feet.

"Wait." Hilda grabbed her hand, pulling her down. "It's the rebels. They want the world to be the way it was when blood ruled, and humans were nothing more than food."

"How do we stop them?"

"I don't know. I don't know who leads them or how they recruit. But their numbers are growing." Hilda grunted, every breath becoming more ragged than the last.

"Shit, you can't wait anymore. You need a doctor now."

"Don't. Don't leave me," she said, grabbing Kelly's hand.

"I won't. I promise. Just hold on."

"Autumn!" Kelly shouted from the doorway. After a moment, she appeared, running toward her. When Autumn reached her, Kelly only pointed in Hilda's direction. Autumn swooped down and tended to her injuries.

Kelly wandered away from the supply closet into the

center of the atrium, her mind buzzing with static, over-loaded with information. She stared at the bodies sprawled across the room, displaying the result of the chaotic struggle. Theo placed a hand on her shoulder.

"Hilda said it was the rebels. They want the world to return to the way it was," she explained, staring unblinkingly at the body in front of her. Forest green scrubs on a petite frame. *Gaia.* Kelly's heart ached. *She didn't see it coming.*

"We will figure it out. I have faith," Theo stated firmly.

"How? In what? The entire council was wiped out," she spat, near hysterics. He grasped her chin and turned her to face him. Looking her deeply in her eyes while retaining his comforting grip.

"I have faith in you. We do not know this as a fact, we only know that the council members that are here were attacked. There are still other members that may be alive." He spoke with unwavering assurance.

"Other members?" she asked suspiciously.

"Yes, there are outpost offices all over the world."

"Why didn't... never mind, it doesn't matter," she said, pinching at the bridge of her nose. She looked around again. "We need to find Will."

"I will find him; you should go see Jonas."

"No, I need to find Will and anyone else that may still be alive," she said sharply.

"Then I will go with you."

CHAPTER
TWENTY-NINE

Each taking one side of the hall, they inspected each room and checked the pulses of anybody they came across. A few survivors made their way to an exam room while Kelly and Theo carried the dead into the atrium and laying them respectfully next to one another. The more ground they covered. The more Kelly's heart grew heavy. As they finished sweeping the final hall, Kelly stood in silent mourning, gazing out at the dead. Theo wrapped his arm around her. In the distance, a faint rattling metal sound reached them, along with a muffled shout. They glanced at each other, then headed toward the noise. It was coming from the cells. Kelly found the guard's body and grabbed the key. As the door swung open, the voice turned into angry shouts.

"Hey, Come on! I'm Hungry!" Evalyn shouted, wrenching on her cell door.

"Evalyn? You're alive?"

"Of course, I'm alive. What the hell is going on? The guards haven't been down here in hours," Evalyn said, puzzled. Kelly unlocked the cell and opened it. Evalyn looked at Theo, then at Kelly.

"Why do you have the key to my cell?"

"The council has been attacked," Theo answered.

"What do you mean, attacked?"

"A group of rebels massacred the council. Out of the almost two hundred occupants, there are around ten that are still alive," Kelly explained.

"Let us get back to the others and we can figure out what to do next," Theo said.

"Take her. I'm going to do one more sweep and I'll catch up," Kelly said.

"If you are not behind me in five minutes, I am coming after you."

"Make it ten."

"Five," Theo insisted. Kelly smiled weakly at him. Then headed off down the surgical corridor. She reached the set of double doors where she had watched Billy take care of Omari and pushed them open. The doors swung shut behind her. She wandered over to one of the rolling sets of drawers and began rooting through and pulling out things they may need. She found a hospital gown. Fashioned it into a makeshift bag and piled all the items she deemed useful in it. Turning around, she spotted Billy propped up against a cabinet.

"Will?" She hurried over to him. He jerked awake.

"What the—" he groaning in pain as he clutched at his leg.

"What happened? Are you okay?"

"Yeah, I think so. My leg is broken. I can barely move. There should be a set of crutches in there," he said, pointing to the cabinet in the corner. Kelly retrieved the crutches, then helped him to his feet.

"What happened?"

"I got a call while I was taking care of Jonas. There was a patient that needed my attention. Said it was an emergency. I told Jonas I would be right back. About ten to fifteen minutes after I got down here, this mass of beings flooded in, taking no prisoners but also not checking to see if people were dead."

"How'd you get away?"

"They hadn't spotted me, so I thought maybe if I got away, I could get back up, let you guys know what you were coming back to."

"How'd you break your leg then?" Kelly asked.

Billy fell silent, then after a moment explained, "I slipped in some water and fell down the stairs to the parking garage. I waited till it was clear, then worked my way back up here. I sat down for a second and must have passed out."

"Aren't your bones supposed to be super strong or something?"

"When I am in my shifted form. When I am in my human form, they are normal. Though I will heal faster."

"That's stupid."

"Yeah, you're telling me," he joked.

"We have all the survivors in an exam room down the other hall."

They headed back down the hall, followed by the clacking of the crutches on tile. As they passed the rows of bodies, Billy stopped.

"They were my friends. I cared about every one of them. I have treated them for..." He broke off.

"I'm sorry for your loss. They will be missed," she said, placing a hand on his back. He wiped the tears from his cheeks and turned his attention down the hall. Slowly making their way to the examination room. Theo stood outside the door like a sentry diligently protecting those inside. "Go ahead in. We are right behind you," she said.

"Glad to see you are okay, Doc." Theo opened the door for him. He held out his hand, stopping Kelly. "I need to talk to you."

"What's wrong?" she asked. He closed the door, his eyes filled with sorrow as he took her hands in his.

"It is Jonas. He passed away while you were doing the last sweep."

Her breath caught in her chest. A strange numbness washed over her. She hadn't known him that long, but he was still her relative, her teacher. She turned her back to him, staring out at the blood-soaked corridor. "Darling, are you alright?" Theo's voice was tender and comforting.

"Why do I keep losing people? I lost Nick, I lost Eric, I lost Jonas, I almost lost you. When does it stop? When will it be safe for the people I care about?" she said. Theo stood there at a loss for words. She knew there was no way to guarantee people's safety; it was just a way of life, but that didn't help soothe her anger. The palpable atmosphere of heartache and desolation was almost too much to bear. Theo stepped forward and caressed Kelly's cheek, wiping away a tear she couldn't contain.

She looked up into his eyes with an expression that begged for solace. Without a word spoken, she threw her arms around his neck and crashed her lips against his. She drank in the warmth of his body as if it were the only thing that could give her life. He responded by crushing her in his embrace, as if trying to protect her from all the anguish that surrounded them. His protection. With his face pressed against hers, he held her close, providing the comfort she so desperately desired. She needed this. She needed his comfort, burying her face into his shoulder, praying for time to stop. Just for a moment. Enough to catch her breath, to find the reason to keep fighting and not to run away.

"Let yourself be weak. I will be your strength until you are ready," he whispered.

"I know." She sniffed. Her eyes landed on the mark on his arm. No longer a dark red patch twisted in an unclear shape. It was nearly identical to hers. "Do you know what this is?" she asked, running her thumb across it.

"No."

"It is an ancient symbol meaning soulmate or eternal love."

"That may be the reason my touch is warm to you," he said.

"I could feel your pain, every cut, every time they touched you with silver, my skin burned with yours."

"It is over now. Do not dwell in the past, for we cannot change it."

Kelly wiped her face and smiled up at him then kissed him once more.

"I am going to take a walk. I need to think," Kelly said.

"You should not go alone; we do not know if it is safe," Theo said.

"I want to see if anything useful about conduits survived the fire. Jonas was working on translating some ancient texts. Maybe he hid them in a safe place or something."

Theo took Kelly's hand in his and they walked away from the packed clinic office. The voices grew fainter as they walked. They said nothing as the metal elevator door clanged shut and the cables groaned into life. Theo simply wrapped his arms around Kelly. When they reached the lobby, she stepped out and led the way to Jonas's house.

Kelly stopped and stared at the smoke-stained entrance. The glass from the windows lay like fresh snow on the street. Black soot marked where the fire had devoured the walls and licked at the timeworn facade. Letting go of Theo's hand, she climbed the three small stairs, the front door open, covered in wet soot and ash. She peered into the front room, the stacks of books and papers now soggy ash bricks of information and stories forever lost. She slowly made her way down the hall, examining the varying shadows left behind. The burnt walls are skeletal remains of what they once were.

The bookshelves of Jonas's study had collapsed, their contents in a chaotic pile of information and debris. Picking up a book from the floor, its original green cover now destroyed, she flipped it over and thumbed through the soggy half-burnt pages. From what remained she figured out it was an encyclopedia containing everything with the letter "P." She tossed it back onto the pile and wandered over to Jonas's desk, the papers that had hidden the surface were now a mess of ash, soot, and water. She ran her hand along the desk, brushing some debris on the floor. Jonas's antique phone sat charred and unusable, its cords melted and frayed. A small glint of light caught her eye. The silver picture frame lay face down on the desk. She lifted it from the surrounding ash. The frame itself was mangled, but the image of the family inside remained intact. Kelly took the photo and slipped it carefully into her pocket. She rooted through the random notes and files in the drawers. *Nothing.* Then headed up the stairs. The stairs groaned and creaked ominously as she transferred her weight, climbing higher into the fragile structure.

"Please be careful, darling," Theo's voice called from the front steps.

"I will."

Once she reached the landing at the top of the stairs, she saw if there was anything salvageable in the library. As she stepped, the floor creaked loudly. She paused and shifted her weight, taking a half step. Just then, the floor let go, crashing to the floor below. Kelly leapt back, tumbling down the stairs.

"Kelly!" Theo shouted. Kelly coughed, waving the cloud of debris from in front of her face.

"I'm right here. I'm okay," she groaned. Getting to her feet, she brushed the ash and dirt from her clothes and looked at the library, now one with the lab. She stepped onto the broken and crooked floor. Kelly shoved the chair Jonas had sat in when he told her about the key into a pile of burnt dictionaries. Underneath, she found a thin metal box roughly the size of a book. As she lifted it, the contents shifted. Turning it over, she found the handle and the small metal locking flap. She propped the box on her knee and pulled on the lid. It didn't budge. She tried again, nothing. *I'll try later. I might just be tired.* She got to her feet, took a final look around, then headed back to the front door. Theo stood by the front steps, looking up at her.

"You could have come in with me," she said.

"No, I think this was something you had to do on your own, but as always, I will be only a shout away. Were you able to find anything?" he said. She held up the metal box and rattled it.

"No luck on getting it open. I'll try again later, maybe with some tools," she said as they headed back toward the council entrance. "Oh, I found this too." She pulled the photo from her pocket and handed it to him. Theo stared at it. Kelly watched as his expression shifted from a sad nostalgia to a happy disconnect. Kelly looked at him, confused.

"That's a wonderful photo of your family," Theo said and, at that moment, Kelly knew how Theo felt inside. Not because of their bond, but because the photo was a small part of his past, not his future. Theo wrapped his arm over her shoulder as they turned out of the small alleyway. Kelly paused at the end of the street and glanced for the last time at the ravaged exterior, when a thought hit her like a freight train. She pictured everything she had just seen in the remains of Jonas's house, the way the fire burned almost everything but also how it didn't, the odd burn patterns on the walls. She stopped.

"I don't think the fire was an accident," she said, her eyes now locked in an intense focus on the scorch marks across the outside.

"Why do you say that?"

"Something doesn't feel right about the way certain things burned." Theo looked at her strangely. "I may have watched one too many documentaries on arson investigation." She shrugged.

"Then what do we do?"

"You, Omari, Fiona, Autumn, and Eli are the only people I know I can trust."

"What about the doc?" Theo asked.

"I want to trust him. Maybe our past is getting in the way, but I don't know yet. We need to find out who did this."

"Should we not find out why first?"

"I think I already know." Kelly glanced around, ensuring they were alone, then continued in a hushed voice. "Before Omari told us you had been captured and what happened in the Black Forest, Jonas sent Will and me to find some kind of key. He believes... believed it to belong to Pandora's box."

"But that is only a legend," Theo interjected.

"Apparently not. According to Jonas, Pandora's box was the original cage that all supernatural beings came from."

"I see."

"We went to some forest in the middle of Ireland, to the birthplace of the first conduit, and we found this medallion. I assume it's the key, but Jonas was sick, and I left before I could find out anything else."

"So, what is our next move, then?"

"I think the only logical thing to do is try to find Pandora's box, but Jonas said he was still trying to decode its location and what it looks like."

"Is it not a box?"

"It could be, but because the legend is so old, it doesn't necessarily mean that. For example, the supposed holy grail everyone pictures as a jeweled goblet when in fact it's more likely to be a very ordinary wooden or clay one, given Jesus's social status. Or in the story of Adam and Eve. Eve bites the apple and gets cast out of the garden of Eden."

"That is not—"

"I'm paraphrasing," Kelly said, waving a hand in the air. "Scholars have debated for years that it wasn't an apple she bit but actually a pomegranate because of an incorrect translation. So, what if Pandora's box isn't an actual box?" She formed an imaginary box with her hands.

"I see," Theo said, rubbing his chin.

"Maybe Autumn has an idea. Let's head back."

THE HUSHED MURMURS of the people inside died off. Autumn was with Fiona, finishing up a bandage on one of the survivors. Hilda had gotten to her feet and a wobbly Billy examined the stitches Autumn had done. Kelly stood in the doorway and jerked her head. They filed into the hallway and closed the door.

"High Councilor, it is good to see you are recovering. I know I left on other than favorable terms."

"Indeed, however, under the circumstances, I think we can leave that in the past. What we need now is a plan," Hilda said.

"I don't think it's safe here anymore. The fire at Jonas's didn't look like an accident. Where is the nearest branch that we can get to?" Kelly asked.

"We have one in every capital city around the globe. We are never all in the same place at the same time," Hilda explained.

"London and Amsterdam are probably the closest," Billy chimed in.

"Is there a way to contact them, see if they can help?" Kelly asked.

"Or if they have been attacked," Evalyn added.

"Thanks for that, Evalyn," Kelly sighed.

"There's a phone in the next office. I'll make the calls," Billy said as he hobbled down the hall. The group fell silent as the notion of no one being around for backup crept into everyone's minds. A few minutes later, the door opened, and Billy motioned for them to join him.

"What did you find out?" Kelly asked.

"Only answer I got was from London. They said to report to Lorelai and let her know everything," Billy recited. Kelly nodded in acknowledgment.

"Do you know what happened to the key? I left it with Jonas when I left for the Black Forest."

"Oh yeah, here, he almost fell asleep with it in his hand and gave it to me for safekeeping," he said, pulling the wad of worn fabric, hiding the medallion out of his pocket and handing it to her. She tucked it into her jacket pocket.

"How do we go about getting to London safely? If we go as a group, we are a larger target. If we separate, who's to say something won't happen?" Kelly said, leaning into the wall and sliding to the floor, running her fingers through her hair as her mind buzzed with thousands of combat scenarios, all ending the same way.

"We don't even know who is in this rebel group. How are we supposed to be on guard against something we don't have a profile for?" Billy asked.

"I think that answers our question for us," Theo said. Kelly and Billy both looked at him, confused. "We travel in one group. There are only a handful of us. You, Omari, Eli, Autumn, Fiona, and I are all fighters that aren't injured," Theo explained.

"I may be injured, but I still have some fight in me," Hilda said.

"How long will it take to heal your leg?" Kelly asked Billy.

"Two days tops." Billy shrugged. She let out an aggravated groan and tapped her head against the wall.

"When is the next flight? If we are going to travel as a group, I don't want to waste any time." She rubbed her face, trying to wipe away the exhaustion taking over. Billy picked up the phone and dialed. After a few moments, someone answered.

"Yes, when is your next flight to Heathrow? Uh-huh, are there seats available? How many? Thank you." Billy returned the receiver to its cradle. "Next flight leaves in two hours, plenty of seats available. We might be scattered throughout the plane, but it's our only choice right now."

"Then so be it," Kelly said, getting to her feet.

"Okay, while we try to get backup, what do we know about the rebel group?"

"The Shadow Syndicate," Evalyn murmured.

"They are only a rumor. There is no way one person could get that kind of following," Theo interjected.

"Well, someone did," Evalyn responded.

"Can someone clarify for those of us under a century old?" Kelly groaned.

"It is said that the Shadow Syndicate wants to restore the earth to its primitive condition. Where vampires and shifters were not relegated to fables but feared and worshiped like gods," Evalyn elucidated.

"It would be impossible to garner that level of support," Hilda pointed out.

"You wouldn't need big numbers if you had some way to immobilize your enemy, like with a gun or some kind of weapon." Billy's suggestion filled the air.

Kelly crossed her arms across her chest, the key pressing into her side, then tensed as she thought of an even more powerful solution. With a hushed whisper, she finished his thought. "Or a cage."

The idea was dark and heavy, but it could provide a solution. The two looked at each other. They both knew that a cage was the answer. One question that remained: what would it take for the Shadow Syndicate to use Pandora's box against them?

CLAIM YOUR FREE STORY

If one hundred and forty-seven years had taught Theo anything it was how to hide.

Eager to live his immortal life on his own terms, Theo Walsh sets out to seek help from the only ally he has—an ancient witch, indebted and powerful.

Torn between his freedom and the possible repercussions of shattering his master's shackles, Theo knows his only options are to break the bond, or die trying.

Download now: shorturl.at/oGHSX

OTHER TITLES BY FAYE TRASK

The Conduit Series

Breaking the Bond (Prequel)

Blood Legacy

Keep up-to-date at

www.fayetrask.com

Milton Keynes UK
Ingram Content Group UK Ltd.
UKHW032048180324
439698UK00004B/299